The Dark Lady

Also by Ian Barclay

The Dragon's Back

Non-fiction

The Facts of the Matter
The 'I' of the Storm
He is Everything to Me
Down with Heaven
He Stoops to Conquer
He Gives His Word
What Jesus thinks about the Church
Death and the Life to Come
Basic Christian Living

Children's book

The Bounty Bible

The Dark Lady

Ian Barclay

BISHOPSGATE PRESS LTD

© Ian Barclay 1996

British Library Cataloguing in Publication Data
Barclay, Ian
The Dark Lady.
   1. English fiction — 20th century.

   I. Title
   823.9´9(F)

ISBN 1 - 85219 - 071 - X

All rights reserved. No part of this publication may be reproduced, stored in a retrieval system or transmitted, in any form or by any means, electronic, mechanical, photocopying, recording or otherwise, without the prior permission of the copyright owner.

All enquiries and requests relevant to this title should be sent to the publishers,

Bishopsgate Press Ltd.,
Bartholomew House,
15, Tonbridge Road,
Hildenborough, Kent TN11 9BH

Printed by Whitstable Litho Printers Ltd.,
Whitstable, Kent

For **Anne Tippett**
Who gave me so much help with the background
of the town and the theatre in
Stratford-upon-Avon
and
John and Susan
In whose beautiful little house
much of this was written.

CONTENTS

Chapter 1   The Tempest 1
Chapter 2   As You Like It 18
Chapter 3   The 'Dark Lady' of the Sonnets..... 32
Chapter 4   Measure For Measure............ 43
Chapter 5   Coriolanus..................... 55
Chapter 6   Love's Labour's Lost 67
Chapter 7   The Comedy of Errors............ 79
Chapter 8   A Midsummer Night's Dream 90
Chapter 9   Much Ado About Nothing 101
Chapter 10 A Winter's Tale................. 114
Chapter 11 Othello 124
Chapter 12 The Taming of the Shrew 134

1: THE TEMPEST

'He's dead.' Anna looked up at Mike with a horrified expression. She had felt Marco's body stiffen, shiver slightly and fall heavily against her. She looked down at the familiar, well tanned features of Marco Devine. He was said to be the most bankable piece of property in Hollywood at the moment and since his arrival in England the papers had been full of endless stories of his rumbustious lifestyle. Hardly a day seemed to go by without one of the tabloids carrying a photograph of him leaving Langan's, or some such place, with yet another beautiful woman on his arm.

Mike bent down and gently closed the actor's eyes, blocking out his rather wild, frightening stare at the ceiling. As he did so, he wondered how anyone could be killed with such apparent ease, without a soul even being aware that a gun was about to be fired. Surely someone must've seen something? He stood again as two ambulance men with a stretcher pushed their way through the crowded bar.

* * * * * *

Everything had happened so quickly. The people in the bar had been momentarily stunned into silence by the unexpected sound of the shot.

Marco Devine's companion — his minder, chauffeur, secretary, whatever you care to call him — had rushed out of the bar in the direction from which it had come. He reappeared almost immediately, looking totally mystified and mumbling to himself, 'There's no one there.' He stooped down and lifted Marco so that he was cradled in his arms, and loosened his tie. An ever-increasing stain of blood began to seep downwards across the front of the actor's shirt; his lips moved. His companion lowered his head as though trying to listen and then straightened up. 'Get a doctor someone quickly. *Quickly.*' The barman who had been polishing glasses behind the bar and who now looked on with horror called, 'I've just done that. I've dialled 999 and the police and an ambulance are on their way. As he spoke, he poured a glass of water from an opened Perrier bottle on the bar and handed it to Anna, 'The gentleman might like some, Miss.' Anna took it and knelt to give it to Marco's friend who shook his head, 'That won't help. He needs a doctor. Could you hold him for a moment and I'll see if I can hurry one up?'

That was how Anna found herself holding Marco Devine. His lips started to move again. By now the room was erupting with noise; everybody was talking at once. Anna jerked her head downwards close to Marco's, anxious to catch whatever he said. It was no more than a hoarse whisper. 'The. . . er. . . d . . . dark lady. . .'

Marco then stiffened, shivered and died.

His minder reappeared with the ambulance men.

Every bit of colour had drained from Anna's face as she announced, 'He's dead.'

'Well, we can't do anything then,' said the man holding the stretcher. 'It's police business now. They'll be here in a second. Are you all right?'

'Just shock, I suppose.'

'Yer, funny thing; very unpredictable.' He pulled a face and shrugged.

The barman brought a stool around from behind the bar, 'There y'are love; you s'down for a moment.'

'Thanks.' Anna perched herself on it. She still had the water in her hand and began to sip it. She gripped the glass with both hands and tried to think. It wasn't possible that a gun had gone off by accident. And if it wasn't a mistake, then it was murder. Thoughts careered through her mind like a torrent of water racing down a mountainside.

Mike reached out to her, 'Are you OK?'

'Yes.'

He took her hand, 'You look awful.'

'I'm alright, just hold me for a moment.'

Mike put his arm around her, 'Not the best start for our first holiday together.'

'Well it isn't.'

'That weekend in Amsterdam didn't count. I meant this to be our real honeymoon.'

They laughed, still holding hands. No wonder the French called it *Maladie d'Amour*.

In spite of a very bloody body close at hand, they seemed totally unaware of anyone else, in fact the room could have been completely empty as far as they were concerned. It was only when the murmur of conversation suddenly dropped, as though someone had turned the sound down, that they became aware of the other people again, and turned to see the police arriving.

'Now, what's happened here?' The officer in plain clothes was the first to speak.

'Someone's been shot,' said the barman.

'Over here,' the minder, directed the policeman's gaze to his feet.

'Good God, it's Marco Devine.'

'I'm afraid it is.'

'You are?'

'Peter Warwick. I look. . . well, I suppose I used to look after him.'

'His minder?'

'Officially his chauffeur. . . but, you could say that.'

The policeman turned to his uniformed companion, 'Sergeant, get the manager and tell him we'll need a room, and set it up for interviews.' As the sergeant turned and hurried away, the senior policeman addressed everyone in the bar, 'My name is Wallace Good, Chief Inspector Wallace Good, and I'm going to need your co-operation. More of my colleagues will be here in a moment and then we'll start taking statements.' The chief inspector was a large blunt Yorkshireman, who was at least three stone over weight, yet seemed to move with the lightness of a dancer. He flicked cigarette ash from the corrugated front of his waistcoat, 'So what happened?'

'There was a shot,' someone near the door volunteered.

'And Hitler had a bloody moustache.' The policeman had had a bad day and sighed with exasperation. 'Look it's going to be a long night and no one's going to get home much before milking time. We could help each other and take some of the pain out of this little conventicle by not stating the obvious. My men'll do that soon enough, you'll see. So, let's start again; who fired the shot?' He turned to the minder. 'Were you near Mr Devine?'

'Yes.'

'What happened?'

'Well... a... a... shot.' The policeman's exasperation made him stutter. He paused, deliberately took a deep breath and steadied himself before he started again, 'And yes, it... it appeared to come from over there.' He pointed towards the doorway, which was the end of a wide passage leading back to the main reception area of the hotel. It was curtained off, and heavy floor-length drapery concealed a pair of swing doors hooked back against the wall. 'I ran into the passage but there was no one there.'

'You're sure?'

'I couldn't see anyone.'

'And...?'

'I went back to Mr Devine.'

'He was dead?'

'No. He was bleeding a lot and I tried to staunch it with a handkerchief. The barman had called for an ambulance, and the lady over there held him while I ran out to reception to hurry things up.'

'Did 'e say anything?'

'Yes.'

'What was that?'

'Well...'

The sergeant noisily reappeared. 'The manager says the big function room is being used by the council for a cocktail party, but we can have the overflow dining-room; it's being set up for interviews. And the Scene of Crime people are here, and they'd like this bar cleared straight away, if that's OK by you, sir?'

Everybody was now ushered into a large empty dining room and the lengthy process of taking statements began.

* * * * * *

Stratford-upon-Avon is normally full of visitors in the summer, and this year was no exception. The Royal Shakespeare Company, trying to balance their books in the face of yet more cuts from the Arts Council, had decided to hold an International Season at the Royal Shakespeare Theatre. The cast, gathered from the four corners of the globe, was headed by Marco Devine, an actor originally from the Philippines who had modelled himself on Richard Burton. He had the same animal magnetism and was able to stand quite still centre stage and hold the attention of every eye in the theatre. He also had Burton's electrifying diction.

One day a Jesuit missionary in Manila had found a group of teenagers pelting an underfed ruffian with rubbish as he declaimed a speech from the battlements of a castle made from discarded cardboard boxes. His last defiant cry as he ran away in tears, his face streaked with filth from the gutter was, 'One day I'll be an actor — you'll see.' That prophecy had long since been fulfiled. The Jesuit, a Welshman with a great love of the English language, taught the young Filipino all the subtleties of speech that come so naturally to the Celts. Before he died, a wealthy parishioner helped him send the young man to the Royal Academy of Dramatic Art in London. Once he was there his teachers sought to polish a voice that had already been trained more than most.

Marco Devine quickly became a star of the London stage. Offers from Hollywood poured in, and he moved to the West Coast of America. Once there, he appeared in a series of mediocre films. Most people felt that he had failed to achieve the greatness that could have been his, but somehow his charisma made even a second-rate film bearable, and his name guaranteed box office success. His decision to return and appear at Stratford had been heralded as an attempt to make a comeback as a serious actor. Most theatre goers were thrilled at the possibility of seeing him on stage again. His name meant that the season was already sold out.

The leading actress chosen for the season was Gloria Glasspole from Jamaica — a perfect foil for Marco. Her

Lady Macbeth, the first to be played at Stratford by a black actress, was said to be stunning. The press were already running stories about the subtleties she had brought to the part even in rehearsal; few had seen or heard anything like it before.

The premiere of what was advertised as a SPECTACULAR INTERNATIONAL SEASON OF SHAKESPEARE was just one night away. The Royal Shakespeare Company had been invited to a cocktail party at The Prince of Denmark Hotel, in Chapel Street, given in their honour by the local town council. Marco Devine found it all rather prissy and had wandered off to look for a man-sized drink and a more appreciative audience. He found both in the Sir Toby Belch Bar, one of the hotel's more public bars on the ground floor.

* * * * * *

By now a WPC was taking Anna to the cordoned-off interview area in the overflow dining room and Anna saw that she was to be questioned by the chief inspector. He was working on some papers as she approached and exhaling a deep breath noisily through his teeth in a sort of whistle, returned them to a file and looked up as she sat down. 'Now, you were with him when he died?'

'That's right.'

'Your name?' He switched on a tape recorder, and clicked a pen ready to write.

'Anna. . . er. . . Main.' Anna just managed to stop herself giving her maiden name. She'd only recently married, and in moments of stress 'Richardson' still came more easily to her lips.

'Mmm.' The big bluff Yorkshire man stroked his chin, 'And you're not local?'

'No we've just arrived.'

'Staying here at The Prince of Denmark?'

Anna shook her head. 'No; we'd just popped in for a meal. My sister has a little house in Bull Street. We're using it for a month. It was too late to buy food, so we came here.'

'You've come for the international season?'

'We'd love to get some tickets, but I shouldn't think there's a chance we will. No. . . we've only been married two months and this is our first real break. My husband has a restaurant in Sussex; he's writing a book of English recipes, and I'm working on a biography of a Sussex artist called Eric Gill.'

'Are we talking about *the* Michael Main?'

'Yes, and I think we know your sergeant. Didn't he work in Sussex? I'm sure he'll give you any information you need about us.'

'Percy Williams, of course; until recently the scourge of the Brighton force — and now we've got 'im, God help us. So take your time, Mrs Main, and tell me what happened.'

'I'm not sure that I really know. Michael and I were sitting at the bar waiting for our food. The shot took everybody by surprise. The barman gave me a glass of water to pass to the man with Mr Devine. . .'

'Peter Warwick?' The chief inspector scowled and let his prejudices show, 'I'm never quite sure what to think of these arty-farty theatrical folk, but when they're not even actors and they go poncing around like Mr Peter bloody Warwick, it really gets on my wick. . .' He stopped himself going further, 'So you gave the water to Peter Warwick?'

'Yes. And he asked me to hold. . . er Mr Devine. It was only then that I realized who it was. Mr Warwick ran out into the passage. And while I was still holding Mr Devine, he went out again to reception to try to get the doctor to hurry up; it was while he was there that the poor man died.'

'Mmm.' The chief inspector pursed his lips and was momentarily lost in thought, 'I think we'd better get your husband and see if he can add anything.'

The police woman was despatched to find him. The chief inspector brought another chair around and put it next to Anna's. He was still standing when the WPC returned with Mike. They shook hands and sat down.

The chief inspector straightened the papers on his blotter, 'I'm sorry I didn't realize who you were. Food writers and restaurant owners are not as easy to recognise as film stars.'

'Fortunately not.'

'But I can see who you are now; you were on Masterchef a few weeks ago?'

'Yes.'

'My wife never misses it, and she reads your column in the Sunday papers. I suppose I enjoy the benefits second hand,' He laughed causing his waistcoat to heave and register at least 5.2 on the Richter scale, 'I could get to feel quite hungry just thinking about it.' Adding gloomily, 'I don't think anyone'll get a plate of blackpudding for their supper tonight.' He turned to the papers on his desk. 'Now, the shooting; what do you remember?'

'Not much; it all happened so quickly. Anna and I were sitting at the bar. There was a shot; I thought it was a firework. And I certainly didn't realize anybody had been hit. Anna was the nearest to the barman, and he gave her a glass of water to take to Mr Warwick, who then asked her to hold Marco Devine. I really didn't twig who it was until you arrived.'

'Wait a moment,' The Yorkshire Terror with the persistence of a dog at a bone still had the scent. 'Just after the shot Mr Warwick ran out into the passage but said there was no one there?'

'Oh. . . yes. . . I'd forgotten that.'

'Anything else?'

'No.'

'You're sure?'

'Yes.'

'Well, thanks for your help. You're both free to go. I don't need to detain you any longer; I would creep away and get some sleep if I were you. I'll get the statements typed up and we'll bring them to Bull Street to be signed; 41a wasn't it?

'That's right. Does anyone know why Mr Devine was shot?

'At this stage we know very little, Mr Main. There's nowt so queer as folk, except queer folk; as we might've said in Yorkshire. I get the feeling that everyone in the bar is going to give us the same information. But *who* did the shooting and *why*, I'm afraid I don't know. However it's our job to find out, and we will — don't you fret.' The chief inspector stood and made an attempt at a smile. The interview was over. They shook hands, the WPC then showed them out of the room into the main reception area of the hotel.

* * * * * *

Mike and Anna had only known each other for a little over a year.

After his first wife had died of cancer Mike decided 'to get away from it all.' He took a long holiday in the Far East, 'to have a quiet think and try to discover what life was about,' was the way he put it. So that the whole experience wasn't too introspective, he set himself the task of looking at Chinese cooking as he travelled.

Initially it had been a sop to salve his conscience; for while most of his body and mind told him that he desperately needed a holiday, a little bit of him - the austere Scottish bit, which he had inherited from his Calvinistic forebears — insisted that he couldn't possibly do absolutely nothing for six whole weeks. So he decided on the research; and what better excuse could there possibly be for travel, if you happen to be a restaurateur?

The whole experience of Chinese cooking, free from the expectations of the European palette, was a revelation to him. He said it was like discovering jazz, when all you'd known was classical music; or finding that the world was round when you'd been convinced it was flat.

When he returned, such was his enthusiasm, some of his customers were concerned that he might stop cooking their favourite dishes and concentrate solely on the cuisine of the East. Mike assured them otherwise, and the menu at The Old Nail Shot Restaurant in the quiet little Sussex village of King's Nympton remained the same, which was the proof of the pudding. One of the bright young things who worked there put it into perspective when he said that all that had happened was a shake of Alistair Little had been added to Elizabeth David. It couldn't be expressed better than that.

Mike and Anna met on his return from the holiday. She had visited King's Nympton, where the restaurant was situated, to advise the local squire on some drawings he had recently acquired. Anna taught history of art at Roedean. Her special interests were the Brighton artists of the early part of the century, particularly the Ditchling school and notably Eric Gill the sculptor and typographer.

* * * * * * *

'Mr Main. . . 'scuse me. . . Mr Main. . . just a minute.' The uniformed policeman, the unmistakable figure of Sergeant Percy Williams, caught up with them in the foyer. The sergeant had almost made a career out of being the most unpromoted man in the Sussex force. He had been beat bobby, community cop, schools liaison officer and then with a sudden surge of study and a good deal of luck, had been promoted. But the stripes looked too heavy for his arm and somehow he was still just a village bobby. He beamed at them, 'I thought it was you. And I said so to the chief, and he said it was. He tells me you're married. Congratulations.' The beam briefly left his face, 'But what are you doing here?'

'We could ask you the same question,' said Anna.

The sergeant laughed, 'Of course you could, but its easier for me to explain. I'm a country policeman really. I decided that months ago, so when I heard that the Warwickshire force were looking for men to run their rural stations, I applied — and here I am; it's as easy as that.'

'But. . .' Anna raised her hands, '. . .Stratford isn't rural. Almost every visitor to England comes here eventually. It's like the crossroads of the world; the centre of the universe.'

Exactly on cue a young Japanese lady came through the main door, leading a bus load of tourists to reception. All that this luckless band of elderly Japanese would see of London would be controlled by what they could see from the comfort of their luxury coach. But on their whirlwind tour of Europe, their one night on English soil would be spent among the genuine Tudor beams of The Prince of Denmark Hotel in Stratford-upon-Avon.

'That's the silly thing really,' explained the sergeant.

'They allowed me to be transferred, but once they heard of my experience in Brighton, they put me on the local crime squad.' He drew himself up to his full height, straightened his tie and announced, 'The chief inspector is my boss.'

'Well we should congratulate you,' said Mike. 'It is good to see you again.'

'And another *murder*?' Percy Williams appeared to put the word in quotation marks and then looking just like Mr Plod he asked inquisitively, 'Are we going to have your help with this one?' Percy Williams was as out of place in the world of real police as a black-faced minstrel would be at a meeting of South Africa's extreme right about to be addressed by Eugene Terre Blanche.

You could almost feel Anna's opposition, and as if to emphasize she was speaking for both of them, she took Mike's arm and pulled him closer, 'We're here for a quiet month's break to do a little writing. There's no way that we're going to get involved. So the answer to your question is a very definite *no*.'

Mike nodded in agreement. 'Please tell the inspector anything he needs to know about us. But, as far as tonight is concerned, we just happened to be here, when Marco Devine was shot — that's all.'

'I'll remember that. Now I'd better get back; there's still loads of work to be done and the Incredible Hulk is in a terrible mood, but I thought I had to come and say "hello".' The sergeant waved his goodbye as he hurried back to the interview room.

Before Mike and Anna could turn to leave, a vivacious young woman swooped down on them. She was wearing a neatly tailored scarlet jacket with shiny brass buttons, a black polo-neck sweater and narrow black trousers. An ivory lace handkerchief spilled downwards across her jacket from a breast pocket. The final part of this stunning creation was a black velvet top hat with a wide, ruched band and bow. Her whole appearance was very theatrical, boldly British and perhaps a little too reminiscent of the Tower of London for Stratford-upon-Avon; but it worked. It was worn by a tall willowy young woman with enormous spectacles perched on the end of a little retroussé nose. She spoke with a commanding, low-timbred voice, 'You poor darlings, you. I've just heard of your part in our tragedy.' She turned to Anna, 'And you were actually holding the Devine One when he died.' She held out her hand, 'I'm Gillian Wykeham-Barnes. I'm the administrator of the Royal Shakespeare Company. I just want you to know how distressed we all are that you've been caught up in this maelstrom of violence. Can you get to the opening night tomorrow? It's hard to think about I know, but in our profession, the show must go on.'

'They tell me you're Mr and Mrs Michael Main.' She turned to Mike, 'Yes, I can see you are. I recognize you from the photograph at the top of your piece in the weekend papers. You must advise us on Elizabethan food — it's all papier mâché here you know, except for the little bit of mashed potato the actors push around their plates. I'll leave some tickets for you at the box office tomorrow — in your name.'

Mike felt he wasn't going to be able to speak unless he said something very quickly. 'That's very kind of you. We were just there when it happened; it could have been anybody.'

'Of course, but it wasn't, was it?' She closed her eyes and held an arched hand on her ample breast. 'It was you, and we're desperately sorry about that, and want to show how sorry we are. About the most precious thing in Stratford at the moment are tickets for tomorrow night. There'll be two for you, at the box office, with our compliments.' It almost seemed as if she was about to curtsy.

'That's very kind of you Miss Wykeham-Barnes,' and

because he couldn't think of anything else to say to this flamboyant creature he added, 'Why on earth would anybody want to kill Marco Devine?'

'Please call me Gillian, please do. We don't know. I suppose our profession is given to jealousy more than most. Actors can be very bitchy towards one another, and often are, but they wouldn't go as far as murder. A little gentle character assassination perhaps, but that's all,' she paused and looked intently at them, 'But Marco did have a thing you know. . .'

'Thing?' echoed Anna.

'Yes.' The torrent of words was on the verge of starting again. 'He loved Shakespeare. . . really he thought about very little else. . . Shakespeare was his life. . . but Marco was one of those people who would argue all night that Shakespeare couldn't possibly have written the plays. . .'

'You're joking,' said Mike.

'No. Oh no. There's so much proof that it was really Francis Bacon, but apparently Bacon didn't want to offend anyone, especially the Queen so it was all done in Shakespeare's name. Earlier this evening at the reception Marco was baiting one of the councillors, a rather obnoxious man called Norris — Bertram Norris. You see whether we like it or not Shakespeare is big business here in Stratford.' She nodded with the sagacity of an old trooper, 'Visitors bring about £50 million into the town every year.'

'Fifty million pounds?' Anna was astonished, 'Each year?'

'Oh easily. Some say much more. And one or two of the town Councillors are concerned, particularly when people like Marco start quoting hard facts like the *Promus*. . .'

'Wait a minute,' said Mike. 'You're going too quickly. . .'

'The *Promus*, it's in the British Museum. It's Francis Bacon's notebook; it's in his handwriting. There is no doubt about it. And it lists many quotations from Shakespeare's plays long before he wrote them. . . but the point is that Marco threatened to take a whole-page advertisement in *The Times*, saying that Shakespeare couldn't possibly have written the plays. Now I don't think he was really going to do it — he was just taunting Bertram Norris — but the last thing the Councillor said as he stormed out of the party in a terrible fury was "I'll kill him".'

'Did he now?' mused Mike.

'Careful, Mike,' said Anna. 'I know that look. You get it when something really interests you. But Mike, we're not going to get involved...'

'Darling, you're absolutely right; we won't.' He turned to Gillian Wykeham-Barnes, 'But I'm interested in the idea that Shakespeare didn't write the plays. Is that really possible?'

'Of course. Look...' She took off her glasses and in one hand whirled them like a propeller until they nearly flew out of her grasp, 'The evidence is quite clear...' At that moment a handful of guests from the cocktail party came through the foyer heading for home. 'Oh, Professor Tombaugh, could you spare a moment?'

A distinguished-looking man with silvery white hair came across. Gillian introduced them, 'Mrs Main, this is Professor Tombaugh... Professor, Mrs Main.' She turned to Mike. 'Mr Main, this is Dr Tombaugh from the United States...'

'Please call me Mike.'

'And you call me Clyde. I'm pleased to meet you Mike and Mrs Main.'

'Anna.'

'Anna.'

Gillian struggled to pick up the thread of the conversation, 'Professor Tombaugh is from Harvard. You probably know that they have a house just over the road. At the moment the professor is researching into the whole question of the authorship of the plays.'

'Miss Wykeham-Barnes was saying...'

'Gillian.'

'...Gillian was saying that there is evidence that Shakespeare didn't write the plays.' Mike added, 'I'm fascinated by that. I thought it was just one or two cranks who had the silly idea that...'

'Well, you may well think I'm a crank.' The American spoke with that gentle New England accent which, some scholars would argue, was probably the one used by Shakespeare. His clothes had the comfortable look associated with senior members of the older universities. His sports jacket was a mixture of colours, reminiscent of the Yorkshire Moors on a bright sunny day in late September. It was elegantly cut, but well worn with two suede patches at the elbows. His corduroy trousers were washed to the pale warm colour of Cotswold stone. The only hint of the American side of the Atlantic was the white buttoned-down shirt and the Timberland loafers. And his face too was very much the New England patrician; aside from his silver hair he could have been the twin brother of George Bush.

'Well Mike, as I say, you may think I'm a crank but, from my perspective, it is becoming increasingly difficult to connect Shakespeare with the plays.'

'But he was born here — we know that.'

'We know a William Shaxbere or Shagspere was born here and probably married Anne Hathaway. But historically the difficulties start when you try linking either of them with some of the buildings mentioned in the guide books.'

'And he became an actor. . .'

'Sure. . . no problem, but actually writing, not *mere* plays, but exquisite masterpieces of the English language?'

Mike noisily emptied a sigh, 'But then why hasn't anyone written about it? Why hasn't someone somewhere, said something?'

'There's probably a book published every year on the Shakespeare conspiracy, but no one seems to take them seriously. . .'

'Why not?'

'That's the big one.'

'Well why?' Mike looked indignant.

'Well. . . there are at least two major areas of vested interest.'

'They are?'

'The English departments of your universities. . .'

'And. . .'

'And the whole *raison d'être* of this little town. If the man who wrote the plays wasn't born here, Stratford-upon-Avon would immediately fall off the edge of the tourist map and would probably never be heard of again. That's why Councillor Norris lost his temper this evening. You have some marvellous old buildings here, but not enough to justify the tourist trade. People come here because Stratford is associated with William Shakespeare playwright. Now look, why don't we discuss this properly sometime? Call me at Harvard House? OK?'

Mike turned to Gillian. 'You mentioned that. . . I'm not sure I know where it is.'

The professor continued, 'It's just across the street. It's a little bit of the old US of A here on English soil. You'll see the Stars and Stripes outside. In Shakespeare's day the house belonged to a butcher called Rogers — Tom Rogers. And among his thirteen children was a daughter called Kathleen and she married John Harvard, who left a legacy of £779 17s 2d for the founding of a university in the United States — now that is real history. There's no doubt about that. Call me some time and we'll discuss it. I must fly. 'Bye now.'

As Mike and Anna said a litany of goodbyes to Gillian, the final guests from the council's party upstairs drifted down and through the foyer. Among them was Peter Warwick, who had rejoined the party after the police had taken his statement. When he saw Mike and Anna he called out in a desultory fashion, 'Hey, thanks for your help. It was kind of you to do what you did. We're all very grateful.'

Finally, apart from two girls beavering away in reception, Mike and Anna were left alone in the lobby of the hotel. The tourists were on their way to bed, the restaurant was about to close, and only one or two people remained with the police.

'We came in here nearly three hours ago to get some food,' said Mike. 'But we haven't had a bite. What would you like to do?'

'Well I'm not hungry now. What about you?'

'I think we should return to Bull Street and call it a day.'

'I agree.' Anna hugged herself to stifle an involuntary shudder, 'I feel cold.' She felt something on her sleeve and looked down to see that her fingers were stained with blood.

'That must've come from Marco Devine.' She shivered again. Mike reached for his handkerchief. 'Keep still for a moment, and I'll wipe it off.'

Anna closed her eyes and held out her hands like a child while Mike wiped at the stain.

'There you are; that's dealt with the worst of it. Now I think we should get you to bed with a hot drink.'

'Thanks. I think that's what I need.'

They stepped outside just as Peter Warwick was easing himself into Marco Devine's rather exotic 1930s car. There was another shot. This time, as it was getting dark, there was a faint but unmistakable muzzle flash from a doorway twenty yards or so up the street. For the second time that evening a gun had been fired. Peter Warwick slumped forward over the steering wheel of the Bugatti Royale. He was dead.

2: AS YOU LIKE IT

The horror of the two killings, the waiting around for the second police interviews meant a night without much sleep for Mike and Anna; even so, Mike rose early the next morning and left Anna undisturbed while he crept downstairs to make some coffee.

As he waited for the kettle to boil he idly looked at a map on the kitchen wall. Under the print, in a copperplate script it said, 'The earliest known map of Stratford-upon Avon, dated 1759 and showing the town much as it was in Shakespeare's day; a centre for marketing corn, malt and livestock.'

Mike noticed that the area to the south of the town, which would include Bull Street, was known as 'the Felden.' He remembered someone had once told him that this was Old English for 'open country.' To the north was 'the Arden,' the woodland setting for As You Like It. The professor's doubts about the identity of Shakespeare filled his mind as he moved to look at three early wood engravings in the breakfast area. Whoever had produced them had no doubt that Shakespeare had written the plays and had left an indelible impression on the town. The first was called, 'Poor market-folks that come to sell their corn' — Henry VI. It showed the market place, and suggested that this was where the young Shakespeare came to study the manners, dress and speech of its tradesmen, farmers, milkmaids and lawyers. The middle print was a cottage herb garden and declared, 'Hot lavender, mints, savory, marjoram; the marigold that goes to bed wi' the sun' — The Winter's Tale. The last was entitled, 'When icicles hang by the wall, and Dick Shepherd blows his nail' — Love's Labour's Lost. It pictured a man making his way through a snow-bound landscape, blowing his hands to keep them warm. Mike looked out of the window; the town was beginning to stir and having finished his coffee, he quietly let himself out the house and set out to look for something for breakfast. Bull Street was near the centre of Stratford and a little more than three hundred yards from The Prince of Denmark Hotel, so a brief walk took him to the shops which were already being patronized by the usual insomniacs and early morning bargain hunters.

* * * * * *

Anna broke off a piece of warm croissant and spread it with butter and marmalade, 'Do you think Marco was killed because of what he thought about Shakespeare?'
'I can't believe that. . .'
'. . .That Shakespeare didn't write the plays?' She frowned.
'No. That Marco was shot because of what he thought. Mind you last night the professor was beginning to convince me that Shakespeare couldn't've written the plays. But I don't believe that's a reason to kill anyone. . .'
'What other reason could there be?'
'I don't know,' Mike shook his head and added black cherry jam to his croissant. 'But then it wasn't only Marco; the other man was shot too.'
'Peter. . .'
'Yes Peter Warwick. Perhaps he heard what Marco said before he died.'
Anna hesitated at the implications of what Mike had just said, 'Well, so did I,' she said quietly.
'When?'
'When I was holding Marco.'
'Why didn't you say something?'
'Nobody asked me and I forgot about it — until now. . .'
'But what was said. . . could lead to the murderer.'
'I suppose so, but are you sure that Peter Warwick didn't say anything? Because if he did, everybody in the bar must've heard?'
'I'm sure he didn't. The chief inspector asked him and he was about to say something when Percy Williams returned, and the subject was dropped.'

'You're sure?'
'Positive.'
'Mmm.'
'If Peter Warwick was killed because of what he heard. . .'
'. . .That means I could be in danger too.'
'It certainly does.' Mike paused and then looked directly at her. 'So what did Marco say?' Anna put down the last piece of croissant, 'So much happened last night. . . I'm not sure. . . I think, yes. I am fairly certain he said, "the dark lady".'
'Meaning?'
'Well. . .'
'Yes?'
'Gloria Glasspole?'
'Why?'
'She's from Jamaica.'
'But if Marco was thinking about Shakespeare, and we know he was last night, why couldn't he have been talking about "the dark lady" of the sonnets?'
'Mmm. I hadn't thought about that. But in any case,' she got up, 'We're not going to get involved,' and started to clear away the breakfast things. They were both lost in thought.

Finally Mike got up from the table and wiped it clean of crumbs. He then did the same for the other kitchen surfaces, and still holding the dishcloth said, 'I suppose the kitchen is my domain, so I'll work here.' He turned to Anna, 'And you could work at the table in the sitting room. Is that all right? I'll get your files from the car?'

'That's OK. I brought them in earlier while you were out getting the croissants.' As an afterthought she added, 'Shall we work until lunchtime?'

'That's a good idea. Then we'll get something to eat, take a little stroll down by the river and pick up the tickets for tonight.'

Soon Mike and Anna were lost in their different projects. On that particular morning he was working on some Starters for his book of classic English recipes. He began with one called 'Mendip Wallfish'. He smiled to himself because it normally came as a surprise when people discovered that the English have relished snails since before Roman times. He described how to take the ordinary garden snail, *Petit Gris*, as they've always done in Priddy in Somerset and simmer them in a stock flavoured with cider. Then, as with Burgundian escargots, filling the shells with butter; but mixing the Priddy butter with fresh dill, fennel, chervil, chives and lemon balm instead of garlic.

Anna had reached the stage in Eric Gill's life when in the 1930s he had been commissioned to produce the two large statues of Ariel and Prospero to stand guard over the porch of the BBC's new headquarters in Portland Place. They were both so absorbed in their work that they didn't even think of stopping for coffee.

* * * * * *

That evening, they made their way to the theatre. It had been a perfect summer's day, and now that the sun was setting a gentle breeze was blowing from the southeast bringing fresher, cooler air, heavily laden with the scent of newly mown grass. They had a little time to spare, so they took the pretty route down Bull Street and past the parish church, Shakespeare's burial place. His tomb, and those of his family, were under the chancel floor in front of the altar As they approached the theatre Mike looked critically at the plain red-brick building, 'I'd forgotten it looked so ugly.'

'But surely, typical of the period,?' Anna shrugged. 'And that must be the Swan theatre in the shell of the original Victorian building.'

'And,' Mike pointed up stream, 'That must be Clopton Bridge.' In the distance swans were swimming hungrily around the famous arches, hoping for food.

The scene outside the theatre suggested Shaftesbury Avenue, or Broadway, or even the Oscar Awards Ceremony in Hollywood, as long black limousines arrived to deposit famous people from the world of stage and screen. Several film crews were working from scaffolded platforms, providing TV pictures for cable and satellite news. Just one presenter was on the ground in front of the theatre, Melvyn Bragg in black tie, was interviewing the more notable arrivals for a future South Bank Show special on LWT.

Approaching the front entrance Mike and Anna had to push their way through a large crowd and convince a security man that their tickets were genuine.

The guest of honour was the Princess of Wales, who was accompanied by the Lord-Lieutenant of the County, Viscount Daventry. The Prime Minister was there with his wife and several members of the cabinet. Mike and Anna eventually found their seats in the balcony surrounded by lesser politicians and TV personalities who on any other occasion would have been in the front row of the stalls.

The plan had been to open the season with a production of Macbeth with Marco Devine playing the title role and Gloria Glasspole his lady. Obviously a last-minute change had to be made, and As You Like It had been substituted.

As the audience gathered, there was an unexpressed feeling that they had come by an error of fate to see the second team perform, that Marco's death had denied them the opportunity of seeing the cream of the world's theatre and that they would have to make do with what they were given by way of consolation.

Once the curtain had risen on John Caird's production set in the thirties, the magic of the theatre took over and the negative feelings quickly vanished. Hanging at the back of the stage was the same giant Thirties Clock that the audience had recently waited under in the foyer. The stage was then dismantled by the actors to reveal lush grass on which they fell asleep. When they awoke, the clock had disappeared and the play had broken through from real time into a world of mist and autumn leaves; a fairy-tale landscape where dreams could come true. By now the audience realised that they were watching an inspired production. When the curtain finally fell on Rosalind's epilogue it was to tumultuous applause. The company took nearly as many curtain calls as they did when Kenneth Branagh played Henry V.

Once the applause was over, the house lights restored and the audience began to move, a young man hurried down the steps of the balcony to invite Mike and Anna to the backstage celebrations. He lead them through a door marked 'private'. and after a series of corridors and staircases, they emerged in the large area behind the proscenium arch, which included the stage with its pronounced rake sloping downwards towards the footlights.

The scenery for As you Like It had been struck and was somewhere above them in the flies. Mike and Anna had been fooled by the glamorous images of the theatre and now found themselves taken aback by the stark austerity of the barn-like space behind the stage. They picked their way through the season's stage furniture; an umbrella like stand of swords ready for use, a table of 'props' laid out with the precision of a surgeon's instruments. Everything was silent and still but gave the impression that at the flick of a switch or the tug of a pulley it could spring back to life.

Now the Princess of Wales was centre stage, which was once more bathed in light as she was introduced to the cast by the theatre's manager. The Princess had obviously enjoyed the show, and appearing to know several of the actors stopped to have a brief word with them.

Gillian Wykeham-Barnes had been hovering at the rear of the royal party, but once she saw Mike and Anna, came over to join them where they were standing just out of the limelight with a group of the theatre's staff and their families.

'You must've had an exhausting day,' said Anna.

'I have. . . Oh I have.' Again it was the deep and beautifully modulated voice. 'I've just finished my last job for the day, getting everyone on stage for the presentation and making sure that they were standing in the right place. They were all trying to up-stage one another — and some actually succeeded. They're like children sometimes y'know. Now,' she smiled at Anna. 'Did you enjoy the evening?'

'It was stunning. So unlike any other As You Like It.

It brought back happy memories of school for me. We had to produce the play after we'd finished our "A" levels — a tall order, but it certainly kept us occupied.'

'Ah. . . I think many of us learn to love or hate Shakespeare at school. Now let me guess.' She paused and closed her eyes for a moment. 'I think you love him?'

'I do, but I don't know him very well.' Anna changed the direction of the conversation. 'Your difficulties today, were they because you changed to As You Like It from Macbeth?'

'Mainly. A decision to change always creates a crisis. It's not just the actors; there's the whole question of costumes and lighting, but the main trouble today was the police. They've swarmed all over us since early morning. I should think everybody has been interviewed at least twice. 'Have they found out why Marco was killed?' queried Mike.

'I don't think so.'

'What do the actors say?'

'Drugs. Well, that's the word going round among the cast. Marco was seen with one or two suspicious characters recently. I thought they were Chinese, but apparently they were from the Philippines. I can't believe that Marco had anything to do with drugs. He was passionate about Shakespeare, and of course he liked a drink, probably a little too much. He was fond of the ladies too; and then there was his obsession with antique cars. If he wasn't talking about Shakespeare, then it was about old cars. I can't imagine him getting mixed up with drugs — It's not Marco, y'know.'

'He certainly had an interesting car,' said Mike.

'The Bugatti — he loved it and garaged it near The Other Place, our third auditorium. I gather the police have been over it with a fine toothcomb but they didn't find anything.'

'Er. . . m,' Mike took a deep breath. 'If I said "the dark lady" to you, what would you say?'

'The dark lady? Oh, "the dark lady of the sonnets?" Now don't ask me her name; that was another of Marco's passions. He felt he knew who she was and he always insisted A.L. Rowse was wrong. I'm afraid I'm not interested in the sonnets. They're far too bawdy for me. Anyway, now I've made sure you've enjoyed the evening, come and have something to eat.' The Princess had left and Miss Wykeham-Barnes now led the way to the backdock, which had been set for a party. The cast and the theatre's staff had already moved in that direction.

At first sight the Jacobean banqueting table appeared to be groaning under the weight of a gargantuan feast. Yet it was soon obvious that the table was a piece of stage furniture which had been set with a boar's head, suckling pigs and enormous barons of beef, all from the 'props' department. Fortunately, there were plenty of real canapés and delicious sandwiches too.

While they were nibbling at these Gillian returned briefly to their side. 'Y'know I'm sometimes amazed at the people in this business. They must be the most neurotic people in the world. . . they worry about every performance. . . where the next job is coming from; and today everything has been overshadowed by the murders. . . and they wonder if they're next on the list. But give'm food and drink and you'd think they had no cares in the world.' She paused before dashing off again, 'Isn't it amazing?'

Half an hour later, having said their goodbyes, Mike and Anna made their way back through the theatre to return to Bull Street. As they did so Anna said, 'I've been thinking, if Marco said "the dark lady", then he must've been referring to the murderer, and surely that must be Gloria Glasspole. When someone's been shot — they're not going to start asking riddles about the sonnets, are they?'

'But. . .'

'Yes?'

'No. . . no. . . you're right.'

'So what d'we do?'

'Tell the police?'

'They're sending the statements round to be signed. We could do it then.'

'Shouldn't we do it sooner?'

'Why?'

'Well, as we said this morning, if Peter Warwick was killed because he knew what Marco said. . . then you're in danger too.'

'Well, I would be if anyone knew, but they don't.'

'I suppose you're right.'

'Of course I am; nobody knows that Marco spoke to me. I just happened to be there and heard him. Everybody else was talking. . . and it was only a whisper.'

'You're right.'

Anna stopped and turned, 'You know what this means, don't you?'

'No?'

'We've become involved, and we said we wouldn't.'

'Mmm. . .'

'I think, I know you well enough to be certain that you won't be able to concentrate until we've cleared this thing up.'

'That's true. I managed to work this morning; we both did. But I was really only developing ideas that I'd already drafted.' After a pause he added 'You're right; my mind keeps going back to the murders and the idea that Shakespeare didn't write the plays. It would be extraordinary wouldn't it, if after all the fuss about Shakespeare here in Stratford someone proved that he didn't actually write the plays? So why don't we spend a few days looking into the whole question of the authorship and then back to work? I'm sure the police'll get the murderer soon; they always do. We might do a bit of amateur sleuthing just to find out a bit more about the "dark lady;" but if we turn up any real clues — its straight to the police. Anything else would be far too dangerous — agreed?'

Anna smiled, 'I think I'd like that. After all, that's how we met — doing a bit of sleuthing — as you call it.'

'Yes,' Mike gave her a gentle kiss. 'Just for a few days, as a distraction from the serious business of writing. But,' He put his finger on the end of her nose to emphasise the point, 'We mustn't forget that art history is your subject and mine's cooking and we don't have the expertise to solve crimes. We just stumbled on the answer last time.'

Anna's mind was already racing ahead, 'So it was Gloria Glasspole. . ?'

'. . .We don't have any evidence for that.'

'But Marco said "the dark lady".'

'Yes, but he could've meant anything. . .'

'But it could be Gloria Glasspole.'

'That's better. But why would a famous actress want to kill Marco. . . and then Peter Warwick? And if she did how did she manage to disappear so quickly without being seen?'

'That's what we've got to find out. What do we know about her?'

'Successful actress. . . Hollywood star. . . nominated for an Oscar . . . leading parts on Broadway,' Mike listed what he had read in the programme.

'Family? Background?'

'Born in Jamaica. I remember reading an article about the International Season recently, it said Glasspole is a well-known name in Jamaica; apparently there was a Governor General called Glasspole. The newspaper linked Gloria with his family.'

'But why should she want to kill Marco?' Having been so certain a few moments ago, Anna was now filled with doubt. 'It doesn't make any sense?'

'Well that's what we've got to find out. Do you really think that she did it?'

Anna's conviction suddenly returned. 'Yes I do, but I don't have any evidence for it, I just feel that it can't be "the dark lady" of the sonnets. How could it be? Honestly,' she added with a hint of exasperation.

By now they were about to step through the main door of the theatre and out into Waterside. The crowds had drifted away; just one or two ardent fans remained hoping to catch a glimpse of their favourite star. Mike held the door for Anna and immediately behind her came Clyde Tombaugh. Mike waved him through as well. 'After you, professor. . .'

'Clyde, please.'

'Clyde.'

'Thanks. Now you're going to call me sometime and come to visit with me at Harvard House? I guess you've discovered where it is?'

All three headed down Sheep Street towards the High Street. 'Well actually,' said Mike, 'I haven't looked yet. I meant to today, but didn't get around to it.'

'Well, it's almost on the corner here, where Chapel Street becomes the High Street, a block down from the Prince of Denmark hotel. L'me show you.' They continued to make their way up Sheep Street.

'Clyde?' Mike hesitated for a moment.

'Yeah?'

'If I was to ask you about "the dark lady," what would you say?'

'Rowse was wrong.'

'What d'you mean?'

'I think Rowse was wrong. Y'see we're back to the old question of authorship again. If Shakespeare wrote the plays, and let's assume for a moment that he did, then Professor Rowse was probably right about the dark lady. But, and again it is a very big but, if he didn't, then Rowse was wrong; It's as simple as that.'

'May I ask you another question?' Again Mike hesitated.

'Sure.'

'Why, when I mention "the dark lady", does everyone assume I'm talking about "the dark lady" of the sonnets?'

'What other dark lady is there?'

'I see what you mean.'

They had reached the corner of the High Street and Sheep Street. Immediately opposite them was a Pizza Hut, probably the most discrete Pizza Hut in the world, hidden as it was among a half-timbered Tudor facade. And four doors away was Harvard House.

'Well there it is,' Clyde pointed. Why don't we meet tomorrow? What time would suit you? Ten-thirtyish?'

'Can you spare the time?'

'Sure. The authorship of the plays is going to take a lifetime of research, so I'll need an excuse for a mid-morning break,' he chuckled. 'My publishers know that they won't get a manuscript out of me for at least another two years. All I have to do at the moment is write a review of tonight's performance for the The New York Times. What'd'ja think about this evening?'

'It was superb. We both enjoyed it,' said Mike, while Anna nodded enthusiastically.

'Superb — I like that. I'm going to entitle my piece "Outrageous stroke of brilliance." I think it was brilliant to set it in the Thirties. We were all depressed by recent events, and more than a little disappointed too, after all the hype, that we weren't going to see "The Devine One and La Stupenda." Then tonight. Wow! In the end it doesn't matter who wrote the plays — they're magnificent. And with a production like tonight, it was fabulous. As you say, superb; I'll vote for that. So we'll meet tomorrow. Goodnight to you both.'

They left the professor by Harvard House and turned back along the deserted High Street. Enjoying the solitude, they had walked only a few yards, when another shot shattered the silence.

It came either from the antique market, or from the Bell Court shopping centre a little further down Ely Street. A clatter of dustbins echoed through the shopping arcade, as someone made a hurried escape through the passageways to one of the other exits.

Instinctively Mike took hold of Anna to shield her. His immediate reaction then was to hurry back to Bull Street and not get involved. But there was a faint, plaintive, muffled cry from the entrance to the shopping area, so they both ran in that direction.

Lights had been switched on in the houses opposite and some of the residents had come out into the street to see what was happening.

They found Gloria Glasspole struggling to one knee. Anna reached her first, 'Are you OK?'

'Geez. . .' Her lips quivered with shock and blood was running down her arm.

Mike hadn't noticed before how stunningly attractive she was; he found every movement mouth dryingly sensual. The blood from her shoulder had soaked one side of her T-shirt and the dampness outlined her breast. Mike found it provocative in a primitive earthy way.

Anna looked towards the wound, 'Apart from that are you OK?'

'Yeah. . . a bit spooked. . . but OK, I guess.'

'We must get you to hospital.'

'Nawh. I'm fine. Just help me back to the hotel.'

'The Prince of Denmark?'

'Yeah.'

The sound of a police car's siren could be heard in the distance, heading their way. Then in no time at all with a screech of rubber and a pulsating blue light it swept into Ely Street. Sergeant Percy Williams jumped from the car. At the same moment a policeman came running through the shopping area. Percy Williams looked at Mike and then to Anna holding Gloria Glasspole, 'Here we go again.' He recognised the actress, 'Someone seems determined to stop the show. At this rate there won't be any actors left by the end of the week. Are you all right?'

'I'm fine. The bullet just clipped my shoulder.'

'What happened?' The sergeant fished for a notebook.

'I was getting a little fresh air. England always appears to be so safe. I'd walked around the block and paused by this book store. . . with Bibles in the window. It reminded me of a shop in Kingston when I was a child. Then there was a shot from. . .' She pointed into the shopping area. 'From down there. . . and he ran off. . . in that direction.' She was still pointing into Bell Court.

'Sergeant,' said the other policeman, 'I ran through from Wood Street and nobody came out that way.'

'I see,' Sergeant Williams paused for a moment as he considered what to do. 'I think we'll get you back to where you're staying, miss.'

'The Prince of Denmark.'

'Well, I'll take you back, and I'll put a constable on the front door for the night. You try and get some sleep and we'll talk in the morning. Do you need a doctor?'

'I've stopped bleeding. We have a company doctor at the hotel. I'll see him as soon as I get back.'

'You're sure?'

'Absolutely.'

'Right, let's get you back to the hotel.' He helped the actress into the police car and turned to Mike and Anna before getting in himself, 'I'll be in touch with you tomorrow.' Then he spoke to the other policeman. 'Stay here until I get someone to relieve you; then we'll cordon the area off and do a proper search as soon as it is daylight.'

Mike and Anna again started to walk in the direction of Bull Street. Anna shivered. 'Well, at least we know that it wasn't Gloria Glasspole. She was nearly the victim just now.'

'You're right.' Mike held her closely, 'So I suppose it's back to "the dark lady" of the sonnets after all?'

3: THE 'DARK LADY' OF THE SONNETS

Back at the house, Anna discovered she was still holding a scarf that belonged to Gloria Glasspole; she realized she had picked it up when she had helped the actress to her feet. It was badly stained and had obviously been used to mop up the blood from her shoulder wound. On the walk back to Bull Street it had soiled the programme that Anna was also carrying. But she managed to sponge it clean, clean enough to paste into the scrapbook she kept for such memorabilia.

The next morning as Mike climbed the stairs to take Anna an early morning coffee, he realised he was destined to do this for the rest of his life; nothing seemed to induce Anna to stir until she had her first, very weak, cup of coffee. So when he arrived at the top of the stairs he was surprised to find her not only awake, but sitting up in bed. 'Not sleeping?'

'I can't. I keep thinking about last night.'

Mike moved the clock on Anna's bedside table and put the tray down. 'When I was in the kitchen just now, I realised that "Chaplinesque" was the word I was looking for last night to describe Rosalind's performance.'

'That's it exactly.' Anna laughed and pulled her knees up under her chin. 'And I won't forget Touchstone's marvellous farmyard impersonations. But. . .' She paused with a hand over her mouth. 'Then, I hear the sound of the shot again. . . the noise of the dustbins. . . the eerie silence. . . Gloria's cry for help. . .' She sighed and shivered, 'It's like a bad dream.'

'A nightmare more like! Three shootings in twenty-four hours is hardly a dream.'

'Of course; it has the same heart stopping night-mareish quality of falling into a bottomless pit as the whole cycle of events begins again.' She paused, 'I suppose the only good thing about last night was that we now know for certain that Gloria couldn't've shot Marco Devine or Peter Warwick.'

'That's right; last night she was certainly the target. What d'you think we should we do?'

'Find out more about Shakespeare's "dark lady"?'

'Where d'we start?'

'We could begin by seeing Clyde Tombaugh; then, we ought to see Councillor Norris. He must be at the top of anyone's list and he obviously feels strongly about Shakespeare too.'

'Of course,' Mike kneaded his forehead with one hand. 'I can't get over the possibility that Shakespeare didn't write the plays — I can hardly think about anything else.' He stood, smiled and put his cup back on the tray. 'I'll shave and bath, then we can get on. I won't be long.'

* * * * * *

Had Mike and Anna been able to see what the police were doing they would have discovered that they were already hard at work, combing the entrance of Bell Court for clues. A line of young constables in white paper dungarees were advancing, four abreast, gathering the most unlikely pieces of rubbish into plastic containers; in case they might reveal something about last night's shooting. Another DC and a sergeant were using a narrow brightly-coloured ribbon to work out the trajectory of a bullet they had found lodged in the frame of a door well within the shopping precinct.

* * * * * *

Just as Mike and Anna were ready to leave, there was a knock at the front door and Mike opened it to find Sgt. Williams on the doorstep.

'I'm glad I've caught you.' He said as he pushed past them, 'We need these statements signed.' He opened his briefcase and put two documents on the table. 'And then we ought to talk about last night.'

'How's Gloria?' Anna was concerned.

'Still asleep. I phoned the hotel and they told me that the doctor gave her a sedative last night; so I'm letting her lie in a bit. I've been to Bell Court to see the Scene of Crime people and I'll go straight on to the hotel after this. By then I hope she'll be awake.' He uncapped his pen and turned to Anna. 'Now would you sign first, please Miss?'

Anna took the pen and sat to read the typed statement.

Mike said, 'Have they found anything in Bell Court?'

'Nothing much; just a bullet. But it doesn't look as though it came from last night's shooting. It was fired in the wrong direction; well within the shopping area, not outside where Miss Glasspole was standing. Forensics are looking at it at the moment. They'll be able to tell us if it was from last night or not.'

Mike frowned, 'Can they really do that from a bullet without a gun?'

'Oh easily.'

When Anna had finished signing, Mike took her place and read through his statement before adding his signature. As he got up, Percy Williams said, 'Now what about last night?'

'There isn't much to tell.' Mike shrugged.

'Just say what happened?'

'We'd said "Goodnight," to an American professor outside Harvard House, and had started to walk back here. Then there was a shot. . .'

'You heard it?'

'Yes. At first we were going to hurry back; we didn't want to get mixed up with anything else. But there was a cry for help. So we ran to. . . er. . . Bell Court.'

'You heard someone running away?'

'Yes. . .'

'Which direction?'

'Through the shops. . .'

'You heard them?'

'Yes. They knocked the dustbins over. . .'

'Forget about the dustbins for a moment, you actually heard someone running away?'

'Yes. . . well. . . no. . . I suppose it was just the dustbins we heard.'

'Thanks. I think that's all I need to know.' Percy Williams started to gather up his papers.

'Before you go,' said Anna, 'There're one or two things we ought to tell you.'

The sergeant was in the process of replacing his notebook in his breast pocket. 'Ah-huh?' Even Percy William's Mr-Plod-like-mind realized that he might be about to hear something new.

'When we got back here,' explained Anna, 'I found that I was still holding a scarf that belonged to Gloria Glasspole. I think I must've picked it up when I helped her to her feet.'

'Well, I could take it to her now?'

'Could you? I'm afraid it's badly stained. I've put it in a bag.' Anna went to the kitchen to get it.

'And there's something else,' said Mike. 'When Anna was holding Marco, he said something just before he died.'

'Did he now.'

Anna returned with a carrier bag, 'Yes I think he said, "the dark lady".'

'Mmm. Well, if he meant Miss Glasspole, he was obviously wrong.'

'Yes. We thought that, but he could've been talking about Shakespeare's dark lady, the "dark lady" of the sonnets.'

'I dunno much about Shakespeare Miss. . .' The sergeant took out a handkerchief and blew his nose, '. . . But I thought'e wrote plays?'

Mike spoke quickly to cover the sergeant's embarrassment. 'He's not really our subject either, but Shakespeare also wrote poems and in at least one he mentioned a "dark lady." So it could've been her that Marco was referring to.'

'Really.' The sergeant didn't seem interested but scribbled something in his note book before he put it away. 'Why didn't you mention it before?'

'It didn't seem important,' said Anna, 'And you didn't ask. . . and Marco also said it to Peter Warwick, which. . .'

'Which is probably why he was shot,' the sergeant finished the sentence, nodding his head in time with the words. 'But I'm sure it won't put you in any danger, or even help us with our enquiries.'

'Why?'

'Well, at the moment we're looking for some young Filipinos who were seen with Marco on the day he died. One of them tried to assault a young lady later that evening. She described him as having "mean" eyes, which has led my boss to think this is all about drugs. To quote him, "Heavy cannabis users have eye trouble, red eyes, small pupils, and reduced intra-ocular pressure" — whatever that is.' The sergeant had moved to the front door and opened it. 'Well it's all grist to the mill, as Old Ilkla Moor Barht-at is fond of saying. I'd better get back. Cheerio.'

When the sergeant had gone, Mike and Anna remained standing for a few moments; neither moved or spoke. Eventually Mike clicked his tongue, 'Tch... drugs. We should've thought about that; Gillian Wykeham-Barnes mentioned them too. So that's what it's all about; drugs. The police must have information they're not sharing with us. So, what do we do? Do we still need to find out about the dark lady?'

'Well, the professor's expecting us, so we've got to see him. And he might give us a lead; we could follow it up. The police could be wrong?'

Mike looked at his watch. 'We've still a few minutes to spare before we're due at Harvard House. would you mind if we walked by the church? I'd like to go there on Sunday. But I'd like a quick look first, to see if it's anything like St. Helen's in London. If it hasn't got any life, we'll go somewhere else.'

'How'll you know if it has life when no one is there?'

'With difficulty.' Mike laughed and turned, 'I suppose if they've got the same hymn books as St Helen's... the books on the bookstall... bibles in the pews... it should be alright.'

They approached Holy Trinity via College Lane. The church was in a neatly-kept garden on the banks of the

Avon south of the theatre and was the epitome of an English parish church.

Mike and Anna discovered from a guide book, that in Shakespeare's day it wasn't in a very good state of repair and that a small ugly building protruded from the east end; a sort of Gothic carbuncle. At one time this had been a choir school, but in the playwright's day it was a charnel-house. In the sixteenth century members of the congregation rented their own pews, with the bailiff and councillors sitting towards the front. When Communion was taken they normally consumed 'eight or ten quarts of claret' at a sitting.

Today the nave is magnificent; stone angels smile down enigmatically from below tall windows and the carved wooden figures in the choir stalls beam with medieval glee.

A young policeman was coming down the path towards them. He hesitated, 'It. . . er is Mr and Mrs Main isn't it?'

'That's right.'

'I thought so. I was one of the DCs taking statements the other night in The Prince of Denmark.'

'Has something happened?'

'No. Everybody in town is a bit jumpy, so we're keeping a high profile to make sure everyone feels secure. The shootings are being treated as a drug-related incident, but we're keeping the main buildings under surveillance, just in case — and I drew the short straw!'

'Sorry?'

'The other guys got the interesting places, and I got the church. Not my cup of tea.' The DC, bored by his duties, was hoping to lure the unsuspecting Mike and Anna into an argument about his least favourite subject.

'You don't like churches?'

'That is putting it mildly — I think they're repulsive.'

Anna winced slightly. 'I don't think I've heard anyone say that before. Sometimes people say the church isn't relevant or intellectually acceptable, but repulsive? D'you really mean that?'

'Yes I do. This is a civilized country; we don't execute murderers; we don't torture people; we don't allow teachers to beat our children. So why should we have a religion that is based on sacrifice? It doesn't make any difference if you kill an animal on an altar, or a person, or even celebrate it — it's sacrifice and that's primitive. It's not worthy of people living in the second half of the twentieth century. That's how I feel anyway. They tell me at HQ that I've got a bee in my bonnet. Well, I mustn't keep you now; it was nice to meet you.' With that he was gone; he made his way back to his car which he had parked near the church gate.

Mike and Anna were silent for a few moments. Then they walked around the inside of the church but hardly noticed anything. They paused in the chancel to look at Shakespeare's memorial and noted his tombstone sunk into the floor.

> Good frend for Iesvs sake forbeare
> To digg the dvst encloased hear;
> Blest be ye man yt spares thes stones
> And cvst be he yt moves my bones

As they came out into the sunlight again, Anna was the first to speak. 'That young policeman has quite thrown me.'

'Me too, but he was wrong.'

'Why's that?'

'He's right about religion and sacrifice; it doesn't really matter whether it's pagan or primitive, Greek or Roman, it's always ugly. And there is an ugly aspect about Christianity too; but Christianity is different.'

'How?'

'Well that's what I've been discovering. When Claire died well actually before that, when she was ill — it was the crucifixion that meant so much to her. She asked me to read about it to her once, and it was then that I started to understand. Christianity is different because the cross is not merely sacrifice — if it was, then it would be as ugly as any other religion. But the basis of Christianity is self-sacrifice; and Divine self-sacrifice at that. As I understand it, it is the self-sacrifice of one who lays down his life to rescue others. Now, that's not ugly, there's even a strange beauty about it which is very moving.'

By now they had reached Harvard House; most of the building was used as a museum. They walked straight in and found Clyde Tombaugh talking to the curator. When he saw them he quickly came over, 'Well, here you are. Right on time. Welcome to this little bit of America on English soil. Why don't we go straight up to my apartment? Let me lead the way.'

Very soon they were seated in a delightful sitting room that reflected the character of its present incumbent. Books seemed to be piled everywhere; most were scholarly tomes. Although the latest Colin Dexter and P.D. James were on a table next to the professor's chair.

He had given Mike and Anna a cup of coffee and had settled back to enjoy a cup of Crabtree & Evelyn's Mango tea. 'It is strange isn't it, most Americans think that the English only drink tea, and you think we only drink coffee. And the reality is that the British are a nation of coffee drinkers, and all the Americans I know love your herb teas. Before Mike and Anna could respond he continued, 'Now, how can I help you understand Mr. William Shakespeare, playwright?'

Mike was glad that at last he could talk about the subject that had engaged his mind, and caught his imagination, over the last twenty-four hours. 'Yesterday you said that there's overwhelming evidence that Shakespeare didn't write the plays. Did you mean that? Is there really evidence.'

'I think so.'

'Where would I find it?' Mike pressed for details.

'You'll need do a little bit of research. . . read someone who can date Shakespeare's plays accurately. Then you must go to the British Library in Bloomsbury to see the Promus, Francis Bacon's notebook.'

'And I'll discover. . ?'

'Well. . . the play you saw last night for example, most scholars date about 1623. And you might remember a quotation in the epilogue, 'Good wine needs no bush.' You can see the same quotation in Bacon's notebook which most people date about 1596 - that is twenty-seven years earlier.'

'That's just one quotation.'

'Sure, but I could give you quotations until lunchtime. In Henry V, dated around 1605 you have "A fool's bolt is soon shot", and the same quotation is in the Promus. Henry IV's "Ill wind which blows no man to good,' also appears in the Promus. Macbeth said, "What's done cannot be undone" — that's also in the Promus. Twelfth Night says, "Thought is free," so does the Promus.'

'Wait a moment,' Mike butted in 'Couldn't it just be that Shakespeare borrowed other people's words?'

Clyde Tombaugh chuckled, 'No, that won't do. There are nearly one hundred straight quotations, and they're not all in English. Some are in Latin.'

Mike didn't reply for a few seconds, 'Mmm. . . you're beginning to convince me. I must look into it.'

'That's all I ask. He's one of your country's giants. The plays are matchless; you'd think that someone would be interested to know why Francis Bacon quoted him nearly a hundred times, at least twenty years before he actually wrote the plays.'

Anna found that she still couldn't get excited about the question of authorship, so she asked, 'And the "dark lady"?'

The professor shrugged, 'Well, that's another problem, but it does depend who wrote the plays. If it was Shakespeare then, as I said last night A. L. Rowse was right, it was most probably Emilia Bassano. But if it was Francis Bacon, then it was Mary Fitton.'

Anna was animated now; she simply wanted to find the murderer. 'Why do they call her the "dark lady"?'

'Because she had raven black eyes, jet black hair, black eyebrows and eyelashes, which the author of the Sonnets found very attractive. He wrote, "Thy black is fairest in my judgement's place." And you must remember that in the Elizabethan Age, most men preferred blondes, or at least ladies with golden-red hair. But Shakespeare, let's call him that for a moment, against all that was fashionable, loved a dark haired woman. To coin a phrase: so far as Shakespeare is concerned, "Gentlemen prefer brunettes".'

'So the "dark lady" was Mary Fitton or Emilia Bassano?'

'Yes... er... yeah, yeah.'

'You don't sound sure.'

'Oh I am. It's just if you were students of mine, I'd expect you to mention Lucy Negro, Abbess de Clerkenwell; Jacqueline Field and Dorothy Soer. But I don't honestly think that any of them were the "dark lady" of the sonnets.'

'So, you're fairly certain it was Mary Fitton or Emilia Bassano.'

'Absolutely. And if you want to check Rowse's arguments, just go to Oxford. It's an Ashmole manuscript.'

'Well,' said Mike, 'We must let you get on. You've been a great help and you've begun to convince me. We must leave you to your work. After all, the sooner you get into print, the sooner the truth will out.'

They all stood. 'That's kind of you to say so,' said the professor. 'But as I said last night, not everyone wants the information made public, and some will do almost anything to suppress it.'

'Anything?'

'Sure.'

'Murder?'

'Indeed. After all, think of what people have done down the centuries to conceal the truth.'

That left Mike and Anna with plenty to think about as they made their way back down the stairs and out into a busy road packed with shoppers and tourists; they headed back towards Bull Street.

Just before they reached the council offices, Anna said, 'Didn't I hear someone say that Councillor Norris had his office near here?'

'Yes, here it is,' Mike had spotted the sign outside a rather ill-kept building between a butcher's shop and an art gallery. The brass plate, desperately in need of polish, announced BERTRAM NORRIS F.C.A. They opened the door to discover that the councillor's suite of offices were just as dilapidated inside as they were outside.

His receptionist was a vivacious little Cockney called

Pauline Chester, who was so lively that she was known to everybody as 'Cheerful Charlie' — 'Charlie' for short.

She bounced chirpily up to the reception as soon as Mike and Anna appeared.

"Allo. How are you then?' She twittered.

Mike was unprepared for this, 'Oh er. . . fine thanks.'

'So what can I do for you?' She tidied the papers on the counter and brushed away the dust with the back of her hand. Mike struggled with the ebullience of the young woman, 'We don't have an appointment, but we wondered if we could see Mr Norris?'

'I'm afraid you can't. It's not that he won't see you, but 'e aint in at the moment — so'e can't.' She looked straight at Mike, 'What didja want'im for?'

Anna realized that Mike was making heavy weather of the conversation. 'Two nights ago Councillor Norris was so upset by Marco Devine that he stormed out of a party saying. . . saying. . . well, saying some rather nasty things about him. It isn't really our business, but we wondered if we could talk to him. . . just for a few moments. . . if he'd be kind enough to see us?'

'I know what'e said because the police have been to see me. As I told them, there was no love lost between Mr Norris and Mr Devine, but I don't think that'e meant that'e was really going to kill'im. He was just very angry — that's all.'

'Can we come back when he's in, and talk to him?' Anna asked quietly. 'When do you expect him back?'

'I dunno. When I come back from the bank 'e had gone. Hang on on a jiffy, I'll see if he's left a note on 'is desk.'

With a busy movement, more like a finch than a sparrow, she twirled and went into the inner room.

There was a pause and then a loud scream, and Charlie reappeared almost immediately with a note in her hands; her face pale with horror.

She stood in the doorway for a few moments and then she said, 'He's done it — it was 'im after all. That's what the note says, that 'e's done it.' She clamped a hand over her mouth as she realized the full implications of the note.

4: MEASURE FOR MEASURE

'May I see?' Mike broke the silence.

Charlie, her mind still rushing through the significance of the note, seemed transfixed, but she managed with one hand still firmly over her mouth, to pull herself together long enough to hand it to Mike.

Anna had walked over to Mike's side so they could read it together.

In large letters, in the centre of a sheet of A4, Bertram Norris had scribbled: 'I'VE DONE IT!' At the bottom of the page he had added an inky flourish which they presumed were his initials.

Mike huffed, 'Well this certainly tells us that he's done something, but I'm pretty sure it wasn't murder.'

The drama had focused their attention on the piece of paper to the exclusion of everything else, so they hadn't heard the door open and the councillor return. His Lancashire voice boomed from behind them, 'I'm glad to hear that somebody has got some bloody sense. Of course, I didn't kill Marco Devine. Although I've felt like it quite often in the last few days, with the sheer arrogance of the fellow. He'd've driven any normal person to murder, I can tell you. Now.' He turned brusquely to Mike poking holes in the air with a jabbing finger. 'I don't think we've met, so you'll have to tell me who you are, and what you want.'

The councillor was a tall lean man with a huge beak nose set in the middle of an unhealthy looking face; it protruded like a cuttle fish bone jutting from a budgerigar cage. Charlie scurried back to her switchboard.

Mike introduced Anna and himself, and explained why they were there.

For a moment Bertram Norris said nothing. He puckered his lips like a flautist and blew a tuneless whistle while he thought over what he had been told.

Finally he grunted and exploded again, 'I don't feel under any obligation to explain my activities to you, or to anyone else. But on the other hand, I don't want to spend the next few days trying to keep you out of my hair, as I've had to do with the police over the past twenty-four hours. So I'll say this: Yes, Marco Devine did upset me, and yes, I did leave a party saying that I was going to kill him. And I might have done so given the opportunity; but I didn't. . .' He paused.

'That's. . .' Mike began.

'And y'were wrong in one particular,' Bertram Norris continued. 'My opposition to Marco Devine had nothing to do with his doubts about the authorship of the plays. You see, I share his belief that Shakespeare didn't write them. And I'm equally certain that it wasn't Francis Bacon.'

'So who d'you think it was?' Mike was intrigued.

'Er. . .' There was a pause. Then the councillor said hurriedly, 'Edward de Vere. . .'

'Who?'

'D. . . de Vere. . .'

'You don't sound very sure?'

'Oh but I am. . . Edward de Vere, Earl of Oxford,' he said emphatically. 'He was responsible for the plays. He was brought up in Burley House in Stamford. And the library acquisitions for that period would've given him all the background he needed,' Again he paused. 'D'you see this,' He brandished his left hand. On the little finger was a large but well worn signet ring. He now held it so that it could be seen, but the engraving was too indistinct to be recognisable. 'It's the de Vere crest. An upheld hand brandishng a spear, shaking a spear — Shake spear! And this.' He fished in an inside pocket for a piece of paper. Having found it, he held it aloft. 'This morning I received a letter about a document that has just come to light, which will prove conclusively that Edward de Vere wrote the plays. Y'see I thought I'd cracked the whole authorship question; that's what the note was about.'

'Well it was obviously about something important,' said Mike. 'But it certainly couldn't've been construed as a confession of murder.'

'I'm glad you say that,' The councillor still sounded curt.

'You didn't 'alf give us a turn, Mr Norris,' said Charlie.

'You concentrate on your work, Charlie m'girl, and I'll see Mr and Mrs Main out.'

As they walked back to the door they were aware that the air was drenched with a heavy scent. In the kitchen Mike had learned that the mute-sense of smell often left him tongue tied and groping for description. But this perfume, for that's what it was, was heavy and feminine.

Once Bertram Norris had opened the door he demanded in his blunt north-country way that they weren't to disturb him again and bid them farewell.

As they continued along Church Street, past the council offices, Anna said, 'Well, I'm confused. Two days ago I thought that Shakespeare had written the plays, but now the list of possible authors seems endless. Who are we to believe, Clyde Tombaugh or Bertram Norris?'

'I don't think it matters.'

'Which one is right?'

'No. Who wrote the plays.'

Anna lost in thought became disheartened, 'So what d'you think we should do?'

'Go to Oxford and try to find the identity of the "dark lady"; or at least confirm that what Clyde Tombaugh thinks is right. The "dark lady" is the only clue we've got; we must concentrate on her.' Mike was adamant.

Anna's enthusiasm was rekindled; she took Mike's hand, 'Let's do it straight away?'

'No, no. . . wait a moment. I think it would be better to set a whole day aside for Oxford — let's do it tomorrow.'

Anna sensed Mike's decision was final, so they walked to The Other Place and managed to get returned tickets for that evening's performance of The Merry Wives of Windsor. Neither of them knew the play, but they soon discovered it to be an immensely enjoyable romping farce. And like Johnson they found it 'too soon at the end'.

* * * * * *

When Anna came down for breakfast the next morning it was to the smell of fried bacon. 'What a delicious smell.'

'You wait until you've tasted them,' said Mike.

Anna sat down and Mike gave her what appeared to be a bacon roll. It had been cut in two, so she picked up one half and tasted it cautiously, 'Mmm,' she paused to enjoy it.

'What is it?'

'It's a non-Jewish, Jewish breakfast.'

'W'd'you mean?'

'They're bagels; I got them yesterday. They freeze marvellously. All I've done is thaw them, cut them in half, and spread them with plenty of cream cheese, a little salt and pepper, and a couple of thick rashers of bacon. Et voila! You have "Big-baconed bagels for breakfast".'

'I'm glad there's only one, or I'd be tempted to have another.'

'Ah now, you mustn't do that; I've got a very special lunch booked for today.'

'I thought there was a little secret planning going on yesterday.' Anna raised an eyebrow, 'I couldn't work out why we didn't go to Oxford straight away.'

'Did you, now?'

'So what've you planned?'

'It's a surprise. I've worked out that it's just a year since you said you would marry me. So I thought we should celebrate.'

'Whoopee,' Anna exclaimed and then suddenly became serious. 'But what should I wear. . . if I don't know where we're going, I don't know what to put on,' she teased.

'My darling you always look marvellous. Wear the jacket you wore last night.'

They were soon on their way. Skirting the Cotswolds, they drove south and passed through Long Compton and Woodstock and finally took the ring road around Oxford to approach the city of honey-coloured buildings and famous spires from the west.

They found a car park that was part of a covered shopping complex; the pedestrian exit led into Pennyfarthing Place. They walked to Carfax Tower and turned left and then followed the length of Cornmarket Street until they spotted the Ionic columns of the Ashmolean Museum.

Climbing the steps, they crossed the courtyard towards the main door. Just inside was a uniformed attendant with the air of a sergeant major. 'Can I help you?' He bristled.

'We'd like to see the manuscript that helped Professor Rowse identify Shakespeare's "dark lady".'

'That's a new one on me, sir.' The sergeant looked at the ceiling and narrowed his eyes, 'Let me see. . . I could show you Guy Fawkes' lantern if you like, or even King Alfred's jewel, but I don't think we keep any manuscripts.'

'I think you do.'

'Why don't I phone the Director and ask him if he'd have a word with you?'

The commissionaire pressed out a number, 'Forgive me for disturbing you, Sir. I have a lady and gentleman here who are looking for a manuscript connected with Shakespeare. Yes. . . of course, Sir. Right you are, thank you.' He put the phone down and looked up at Mike. 'Could you hang on for a moment? He's coming out.'

A smallish gentleman came through from the back. He was dressed in a sober dark blue pinstriped suit, more like a banker than someone from the antiquities department of a university. 'You're looking for a manuscript?'

'Yes. The one that helped Dr. Rowse. . . the historian. . . identify Shakespeare's "dark lady".'

'I'm afraid we don't have it.'

'An American professor in Stratford said it was in the Ashmol. . .'

'Ah now I see what has happened. I think whoever-it-was who spoke to you in Stratford, probably said it was "an Ashmole manuscript". . .'

'But. . .'

'Elias Ashmole was our founder. He opened the original museum for the curiosities collected by the naturalist John Tradescant. We don't have any manuscripts here, you'll find them in the Bodleian.'

'The Bodleian?'

'Yes. The Old Library next to the Radcliffe Camera. I'm sure they'll be able to help you.'

'Thank you.'

Once outside Mike and Anna headed along Broad Street past Blackwells Bookshop, and turned right at the Sheldonian towards the Old Library. After they had waited their turn in the queue an attendant gave them his full attention. 'We'd like to see a manuscript, please?'

'Are you a member of the university?'

'No.'

'Then you'll need a reader's ticket. You can apply for one across the quad in the admission's office.'

'We only want to confirm a name.'

'I'm afraid you'll still need a reader's ticket to see the manuscript. . . Oh there's one of the gentlemen from the duty office. Perhaps he'll explain the procedure.'

A young man in a tweed jacket came over. 'I gather you've got a problem?'

'We're trying to find out about Shakespeare's "dark lady". Professor Rowse said it's someone called "Bassano". We just wanted to check that.'

'You're in luck. Dr Rowse was my tutor; it's the Simon Forman manuscript you want; do you have a reader's ticket?'

'No. But we only want to confirm the name.'

'Well, I can tell you it's Bassano. . . Emilia Bassano.'

'Are there other names?'

'Yes, but according to most scholars at the moment she's the leading contender.'

'I think that's all we need to know. That's a great help. Thank you.'

Once outside Mike said, 'So Clyde Tombaugh was right. It was Emilia Bassano. Now let's get the car and go for lunch.'

Anna looked surprised. 'Aren't we lunching in

Oxford? I thought as we were here we'd be going to the Randolph or Bath Place?'

'Ah did you? That means you haven't guessed. . . good.'

They found the car and took the Wheatley Road over Magdalen Bridge; once clear of the city they drove through a pleasant patchwork of countryside towards the Chiltern Hills that appeared to act as a barrier preventing a whole collection of Wycombs from slipping down onto the farmlands of Oxfordshire.

Just before they reached the motorway, Mike said, 'Here we are.'

'Of course,' Anna exclaimed, 'Le Manoir aux Quat' Saisons.'

'And, what Jonathan Meades in *The Times* called, "the best cooking in Britain".'

'What a marvellous way to celebrate.'

'The only way,' said Mike. 'If food be the music of love, play on. . .'

They laughed as Mike manoeuvred the car into a parking space in front of a Jacobean Manor.

Inside they declined an aperitif and were shown straight to the dining room. Although they had hardly noticed it, the events of the last few days had cast a shadow over everything, but now the lightness and comfort of the room dispelled any sense of heaviness. Despite the grey day, perhaps even because of it, Le Manoir's garden room was full of life and gentle hues. Everywhere flowers stood, tumbled, cascaded with colour; each table was a platform for polished glasses standing to attention and reflecting the miniature pink roses they surrounded. Anna felt she would be satisfied simply to sit and look, let alone enjoy the cooking. Through the window, elegant lawns stretched to what must have been the kitchen garden, its wall hiding the more prosaic treasures or perhaps guarding the secrets of the food they were about to enjoy. Once seated they began to study Francois Duvall's suggestions for lunch.

'You know,' Mike looked at the menu. 'This really is music. For the overture I'm going to have the wild mushrooms and sweetbreads; followed by the symphony of roast scallops and John Dory on a bed of seaweed.'

Anna was thoughtful for a few more moments, 'Yes, it is music, But I see it a little differently. 'I'm going to start with Beethoven, the salad, and then continue with the Chopin, the ris de veau.'

For the next few moments they were lost in a playful badinage debating whether the food was the composer or the composition. In the end they agreed to differ, but both saw that Francois Duvall's task, as Mike's at The Old Nail Shot Restaurant was to act as the orchestral conductor bringing together the whole range of tastes. And they agreed that it was often difficult for the chef to enhance the subtle tastes rather than letting them be hidden in the more robust flavours.

The wine waiter had filled their glasses with *Veuve Cliquot Ponsardin*. With a mock seriousness Mike said, 'Now if we had been talking about wine and not food I'd've said this was Handel.' He tasted it, 'Mmm... *pure* Handel... Handel at his best.'

The conversation now moved to wine and music; and they argued whether the chateaux or the cepage ought to bear the composer's name.

Around them parties of businessmen sought to impress their clients; at each table the guests concentrated on entertaining or on being entertained.

When the waiter had cleared away their main course, Mike took Anna's hand. 'I'm not very good at this,' He paused. 'If speaking was like cooking, I'd be better at it.' He hesitated again, 'I just wanted to say that I love you and to thank you for the first year; it's been marvellous.' He raised his glass, 'May every year be as happy as this one.'

'Amen to that.' Anna looked at Mike, her eyes shone. 'Are you glad you married me?'

'Blissfully. I couldn't be happier. And you?'

'Oh, I can't put it into words. I thought I was happy before we met. Now I sometimes feel as if I've woken from a long sleep. Every part my life has become richer and fuller, my work... love... art... music... wine, in fact... everything...'

They were discretely left undisturbed until the conversation had returned to more mundane matters.

Eventually Mike said, 'Shall we give the pudding a miss and go straight on to coffee. What about a brandy?'

Anna was still bright-eyed with enjoyment. 'Not for me, but you have one and I'll drive.'

Over coffee, they began to make plans for the next move. Mike took an old envelope from his pocket and wrote on it 'Emilia Bassano.' 'I think we've got to presume that Shakespeare's our man and we're looking for his "dark lady." So, I suggest we go back and and ask Gillian if there's an Emilia Bassano in the company.'

'Shouldn't we hedge our bets? Clyde Tombaugh, and Marco by all accounts, were both convinced that the plays were written by Francis Bacon so shouldn't we be looking for Mary Fitton as well?'

'Well there's no harm in asking about both.' Mike added Mary Fitton's name to his notes, then looked at his watch. 'I don't think Gillian works office hours, but if she does we could still catch her. Shall we try?'

The waiter had put a leather folder on the table next to Mike, he reached for his wallet as he opened it. The piece of paper inside was absolutely blank. On a small business card was a note:

Sorry I'm not here today. I heard that you'd booked a table. Enjoy your lunch and regard it as a belated Wedding present.
                              Aye,
                                      Francois

Mike showed it to Anna.

'How very sweet.'

'Well we've worked together so often in the past I'd do the same for him if he came to the Old Nail Shot.'

Mike slipped a banknote into the folder for the staff. They departed and were soon on the M40 heading back towards Stratford. The route wasn't as picturesque as the morning's drive, but it took half the time.

Entering the theatre they climbed the echoing uncarpeted stairs to the administrator's office.

Reaching her floor, they found Gillian saying goodbye to three Japanese businessmen, who were taking their leave with a series of low bows. Mike and Anna stood to one side to let them pass and waited until they had vanished down the stairwell before making a move.

Gillian shrugged. 'Aren't they delightfully polite?'

'And interested in Shakespeare?' Anna was intrigued.

'Oh certainly. Japan has just hosted the Fifth World Shakespearian Congress. Seiya Tamura, the Managing Director of the Globe Theatre in Tokyo, told me the other day that Shakespeare... let me start again... Shekusupia is the most popular playwright in Japan at the moment.'

'Shekusupia?'

'Ah-huh.'

'I'm impressed.'

'So you should be.' She then gave the game away with a laugh, 'Actually it's the only Japanese word I know. Now... how can I help?'

'Well we want to know if there is anyone in the company called Emilia Bassano or Mary Fitton?'

'That's very easy to answer. No.'

'Are you sure?'

'Absolutely.'

Mike's heart sank; he had been convinced that there was a connection between one of the names and the murderer. The confirmation of the name at the Bodleian and the celebration lunch had lifted his spirits. But now his hopes were dashed; the only comfort was the faint possibility that Gillian had overlooked someone. 'Is there a list of the company anywhere?'

'Yes. But it's the same as the one printed in the programmes; exactly the same.'

'Is everyone on the list?' 'Yes... *yes*.'

'All ancillary staff... people in the office... in administration?'

'There are one or two very junior girls, but none called Fitton or Bassano.'

'Has anyone left recently?' Mike was convinced that there was a connection somewhere.

'Contracts run for the season; so people are unlikely to come and go in between.'

'Yes, but has anyone left?'

'No. Well, yes there was one girl from the Philippines called Emily Lanier. She didn't gel with the rest of the company. She was lucky; her agent managed to get her a part in a TV series and she's gone to London.'

'Emily?'

'Yes, it was Emily I'm afraid, not Emilia, I'm absolutely certain about that; and Lanier, very definitely Lanier; I saw her passport.'

A Wagnerian gloom descended on the room. Mike sighed and moved to look out of the window at the river. They were both bitterly disappointed. In the end, Anna decided that the only thing that could be done was to change the subject,

'We saw Councillor Norris yesterday.' she said. 'What a funny man!'

Gillian made a laughing cough, 'I'm not sure I'd call him funny. But I know what you mean. Has he simmered down yet?'

'A little. But, he wasn't angry about the idea of Francis Bacon writing the plays. He thinks they were written by Edward de Vere.'

'Oh, he's one of those.'

'One. . .?'

'Well every time we put on The Merry Wives, there's always a little group of people who espouse the idea that the author was the Earl of Oxford.'

'Why's that?'

'In The Merry. . .'

'We saw it last night.'

'Well, you'll remember in Act 2 a character tries to trap Falstaff. He's called Ford. Some people think it's a play on "Ox-ford". Because he enters disguised as Master Brook, which if transformed into "Spring" and Latinized becomes Ver. And you know the Earl of Oxford's name was Edward de Vere. . . I think it's all too far-fetched.'

Anna wanted to clear everything on her mind about the councillor. 'Mr Norris said that the de Vere family crest is a spear being shaken — shake spear — have you heard that?'

'Yes, I have, but it's not true. I phoned the College of Arms about it once and the herald on duty told me that neither the de Vere coat of arms nor the crest has anything to do with Shakespeare.'

'Mmm.'

'I'm afraid I haven't been very helpful. But I'm not sure what you're looking for.'

'Well, before Marco Devine died he said, "the dark lady", and we think there's a connection between Shakespeare's "dark lady" and the murder of Marco Devine and Peter Warwick, and the attempted killing of Gloria Glasspole.'

'Do the police know?'

'Of course.'

Gillian inhaled deeply and shrugged, 'Well I wish I could help, but I can't think of any way I could.'

Once more Mike and Anna found themselves outside and walking back towards Bull Street. At the corner of Chapel Lane and Chapel Street they met Clyde Tombaugh and Gloria Glasspole on their way to Harvard House.

Clyde Tombaugh said, 'How's the search for the "dark lady" going?'

'We've just been to Oxford to the Ashmolean. . .'

'The Ashmole manuscripts are in the Bodleian. . .'

'We've discovered that, and the people there were very helpful. We came back to see if we could match the names with anyone in the company. . .'

'. . .And there was no one called Fitton or Lanier. . .'

'Lanier? You mean Bassano?'

'Well it doesn't matter what you call her. She was born Emilia Bassano, the daughter of Alfonso Bassano, the Queen's musician. But she became pregnant and another court musician, called Lanier married her. Some say that Shakespeare was the father of her child.'

'So it's Lanier that we're looking for?' Mike raised his hands with glee, clenched his fist and punched the air.

'D'you know, I think we've got our first real clue — Miss Lanier, is the "dark lady". Boy. . . we've got to find her.'

5: CORIOLANUS

Gillian Wykeham-Barnes doodled fretfully on a pad as she sat hunched over the telephone in her office. She had listed all the jobs that needed to be done. From the posters on the walls she was overlooked by characters from the successful RSC shows of the past. Antony Sher, as his inimitable Richard III, stared down at her; as did Nicholas Nickleby. Above her desk was a beautiful small oil painting of Lady Godiva riding through Coventry in 1040, covered only by her long flowing hair.

The call was from her opposite number at the Barbican Theatre who was struggling to arrange a tour for twenty American 'Friends of the RSC.' They wanted to see all the plays currently being performed by the company, including those not in the RSC's own auditoria, such as Les Miserables at the Palace Theatre in London.

The office was normally a place of immense activity. And as if to bear witness to this every available space, including the floor, was scattered with papers, programmes and all the debris of a working theatre which at any one time juggles up to fifteen major productions in repertoire.

Apart from the hectic figure of Miss Wykeham-Barnes, who had now stopped scribbling, the only movement in the office was the tiny winking rectangle of light on a computer screen. Had she looked at it, she would have realized that its pulse matched the furious rhythm of her own heart in frustration at not being able to get on with her work. It was inevitable that once the call was over, and she had returned to her tasks, it would ring again immediately. It did. She picked it up with a brusque and harassed, 'Yes.'

Once she realized who it was, her tone quickly changed, 'Mike. I'm so sorry. . . please forgive me, it's been one of those wretched days. . . of course. . . any time. What can I do? Yes... just a moment,' she reached for a heavy volume of Spotlight, took down 'Actresses L-Z' and flicked through the pages until she found what she wanted. 'Here we are.' She read the words under a photograph of an attractive dark-haired young woman with gentle oriental features. 'Emily Lanier, five foot two... brown eyes... agents: Bill Tizzard Associates... and there's a phone number.' She read it out to him.

There was a pause and Gillian found herself nodding in agreement with what Mike was saying. Then she said, 'So you think it's her? Well, I can see that, but she was very quiet. Mmm. Well I find it difficult to imagine that she had anything to do with the murders... of course you must, I understand that. I'm sure she will see you, but if you have any difficulty mention my name... good luck... 'bye.'

Gillian's irritability suddenly vanished. The list was still in front of her, but she made no attempt to get on with it. The computer's cursor continued to flash, but it no longer matched her frustration. In fact, her exasperation had vanished and she now sat serenely lost in thought.

* * * * * *

Mike phoned Emily Lanier and found that she was staying at her boyfriend's house in South London. They arranged to meet the following morning. Mike made a mental note that it was the boyfriend's number listed in Spotlight.

Mike and Anna decided to take the train to London. And as Oxford appeared to be the best place to catch the Intercity into Paddington, they drove there the next morning. Failing to allow time for the almost impossible task of parking, they just managed to catch the 10 o'clock train by a whisker. As they collapsed on opposite sides of a table in an open carriage, Mike was chuckling.

'I must've missed something.' Anna took off her jacket and folded it carefully before putting it up on the rack and sitting down.

'Did you see the elderly man who got off?'

'Not properly.'
'He looked like my old classics master. . .'
'And. . ?'
'Well. . . there is a story that he once asked for, "a first person singular to Oxford".'
'That can't be true.'
'You're right. . . but it's a good story.'
'What are we going to do when we get to London?'
'Take the tube to Kennington. . .'
'No, I mean, what are we going to do about Emily Lanier?'
'Find out if she had any reason for killing Marco Devine.'
'But. . . we can't ask her; not just like that?'
'No, but we could try to find out if she'd had more than a passing friendship with Marco? See if she's hiding anything. . . and we could ask if the "dark lady" meant anything to her. Unless she's a completely hardened criminal, she must give something away.'

Anna cupped her chin in her hands as she leant on the table and looked at Mike.

'What are you thinking?'
'The Gatwick Express. . .'
'The Gatwick Express. . ?'
'Yes, that's when we started to get to know each other; remember?'
'Mmm. That must have been the first time that I said I loved you.'

Mike bit his lip as he thought, 'How strange. . .'
'. . .That we fell in love?'
'No. . . the journey from Gatwick silly; so much has happened since. It feels a lifetime away.'

Anna looked out of the window at the Oxfordshire countryside as it swept by. The train passed an industrial site, and a dark building momentarily caused a young girl who was walking through the train to be reflected in the window. Anna started to think about Emily Lanier. She was curious to know what she was like, and if she knew why they wanted to see her. If she was the murderer she must feel the net was beginning to tighten.

The rest of the journey passed quickly and when they arrived at Paddington they took the District Line to Embankment and then the Northern Line to Kennington. They had been told to turn left into the main road outside the tube station, then right by the art college into Cleaver Square. Somehow they hadn't expected such a beautiful Edwardian Square in that part of London, yet here it was, light and airy and free of litter.

They found the house they wanted in the far right-hand corner of the square; just two or three doors down from The Prince of Wales, a wisteria covered pub with tables outside.

Emily Lanier answered the door bell. She gave them a warm smile and invited them in suggesting that they went up to the drawing room on the first floor. As the actress led the way, Anna noticed she was simply dressed in faded blue jeans and a T-shirt. But as they came up to the light of the first floor, a second glance revealed that the jeans were beautifully cut blue suede, and the simple white T-shirt was raw silk.

It was an elegant drawing room and again, deceptively simple: an immaculately polished floor was scattered with old rugs and at the far end of the room, floor-length windows looked out over the square. The deep, comfortable armchairs and sofa were upholstered in the palest pink silk and scattered with cushions in a contrasting dark green. On one side of the fireplace was an autumn landscape by Sesshu, who specialized in Sumi-e — stunning monochrome ink drawings. Balancing it in the other recess was a landscape by Mononobu which had the bold brushwork, blurred outlines, and angular forms characteristic of the Kano school founded by his father.

In the corner by the door was a full suit of scale armour with the individual plates made of horn, lacquer and leather. The helmet had wing-like projections on either side and was embellished with a green and gold dragon on top. On the wall opposite the fireplace were shelves displaying bronzes and terracottas, including Haniwa figurines and a Dotaku

— a bell-shaped bronze. On the remaining wall was a collection of swords by Masamune of Sagami and some beautifully intricate and individually crafted sword guards, or tsuba.

The room took Anna's breath away, 'What a beautiful room!'

'Thank you. . . please sit down.'

Once they were seated a Filipino maid appeared and served coffee; as she retreated, Emily Lanier asked, 'How can I help?'

'We've come from Stratford. . . ' Mike hesitated. He looked at the actress, who was such a slight figure that he could hardly imagine her holding a gun, let alone shooting one. He found himself making a ridiculously silly remark, 'And there've been. . . er. . . some murders.' He could've kicked himself for such a fatuous comment.

'The papers have been full of little else. . .'

'Of course. . .'

Mike's reticence gave Emily Lanier the opportunity to speak as she offered them biscuits, 'Marco was a gift to journalism; he created publicity wherever he went. It's not surprising that he upset someone. But to kill Peter, his dresser — that must've been a shock for everyone.'

'There's a pattern. . .' Mike decided he had to be firm.

'. . .And there's Gloria Glasspole,' said Anna.

'Killed?' Emily Lanier looked horrified.

'No. Oh *no*. But she had a lucky escape. The bullet just grazed her shoulder; another few inches and it would have been fatal.'

'The papers haven't mentioned. . .'

'There've only been the two murders, but it was a serious attempt on Gloria's life,' Mike got going at last. 'I'm surprised it hasn't been in the papers. I'm sure it hasn't been officially withheld. Just before Marco died he said, "the dark lady" and we think he was trying to tell us something — even who the killer was.'

'He must've meant Gloria Glasspole. She's. . .'

'But what about Shakespeare's "dark lady"?'

'Nobody really knows who she was.' The actress shrugged.

'They do. It was... Emilia Lanier!'

Suddenly the room was very still, as if someone had frozen the frame of a video film. Mike and Anna were looking at the actress, who had been about to speak but had stopped in mid gesture with her mouth open.

Eventually Mike said, 'She was born Emilia Bassano, but married a man called Lanier, a musician in the Court of Elizabeth I, so she became Emilia Lanier. Shakespeare was probably the father of her child.'

'How strange...' said Emily, 'but its... er... coincidence. You don't think I killed..? you do? That's ridiculous! Why should I want to kill Marco? Why should anyone want to kill him?'

'That's what we want to find out,' said Anna.

'Why did you leave Stratford?' Mike probed.

'It was the wrong place for me.'

'In what way?'

'I'm not a classical actress. I didn't find Shakespeare easy. Frankly, I don't know what he's talking about half the time. Blank verse is beyond me; I'm not really a stage actress. In a thousand years I couldn't project my voice, as they wanted me to. I realized that, and eventually they did too.'

'Mmm...' Mike looked at her. He decided there was no way that she could be the killer unless she was a much better actress than they realized. 'Marco originally came from the Philippines. Would it be very rude to ask where you're from?'

'I'm Eurasian. I came from the Far East. I'd've thought that was obvious. My mother was from the Philippines. I don't know who my father was.'

'Did you know Marco in the Philippines?'

'No.' She shook her head and smiled for the first time since she had welcomed them. 'We both came from the Philippines, but I must've been in primary school when he left. In any case he grew up in the slums; he was from Smoky Mountain.'

There seemed to be little point in continuing. Mike was convinced that she couldn't have been involved in the shootings, so he got to his feet. 'Well, thanks for seeing us.'

'I wish I could've been more help. Do you really think I killed Marco?'

'I suppose the answer is "no." But, Marco said "the dark lady", and Shakespeare's dark lady was called Emilia Lanier and you're Emily Lanier. . . it all seemed to add up. . .'

'Well, let me assure you — I didn't kill him.'

'I believe that. . .'

'And I believe it too,' Anna got up and walked to the shelves opposite the fireplace. She bent down to look at a netsuke; a bear playing with a ball, carved from a walrus tusk. Looking around, she couldn't help exclaiming, 'You really have the most stunning house.'

'Thank you. You seem to appreciate Japanese art. That's not very common among Europeans.'

'I enjoy whatever is beautiful,' said Anna. 'I studied history of art, but only did a term on Japanese artists, so I know very little. Is that a Sesshu to the left of the fireplace? I'm not certain?'

'Very good; it is. He was a fifteenth-century Zen priest and painter. On the other side it's a Motonobu. . .'

'Of course, Motonobu, sixteenth-century.'

'Excellent. You obviously know more than most people. You might like to know that my boyfriend is Japanese and has a gallery in Knightsbridge that specializes in Japanese art.'

'What's it called?'

'Yamashita. . . Gallery Yamashita. . . he's Jimmy Yamashita. That's his father in the photograph on the table. He was a famous general.'

They both turned to look, but Anna quickly turned back to the netsuke, which she found much more interesting. This time she picked up a little ivory fox that had just caught a chicken. 'It's beautiful. . . they're all very, very, beautiful.'

'And no doubt very expensive,' said Mike ruefully. He turned to Emily. 'I've discovered after only a few weeks of marriage, that my wife likes beautiful things. She also has remarkably good taste, because whatever she likes is invariably the most expensive. Would you excuse us - I need to get her away from here quickly before she falls in love with one of those beautiful little. . .'

Netsuke.'

'. . .Precisely. Before she falls in love with one and wants one for herself.' They laughed as they went down stairs and said goodbye.

Once outside, Mike and Anna decided to lunch at the pub in the corner of the square. Mike left Anna sitting in the sun, while he went to forage for something inside. Once in the bar he discovered that The Prince of Wales was patronized by what appeared to be the entire staff and students of the Art College on the corner of Kennington Park Road.

The bar was full of people attired in the most exotic clothes, especially the men, who were strutting around like peacocks. There was a debate at one table about the standing of Lucien Freud as an artist; in the end it was agreed that he was probably the greatest living artist of the human form. A slightly older man, a tutor by the look of him, was filling a small black sketchbook with lightning drawings of those around him. Within reach he had an untouched glass of wine and a sandwich; obviously his meat and drink was to record the social habits of others. Near the bar was a stunning African girl, obviously a model from her bean pole figure and the fact that she was keeping a collection of male hangers-on amused with stories of the goings-on-behind-the scenes in the world of *haute couture.*

Once served Mike pushed his way back through the crowded bar with two glasses of wine and two Stilton ploughman's. While they enjoyed these and Mike's description of the arty crowd inside, they started to make plans for the afternoon.

Anna wanted to look at Paul Costello's shop in New Bond Street. While he enjoyed seeing Anna in the clothes she wore, searching the shops for them was not his cup of tea. So, as it was just around the corner, Mike decided he would visit the Imperial War Museum.

The faded black and white photograph of Jimmy Yamashita's father, in a Japanese field uniform of the

World War II, continued to nag him. Mike wasn't sure why, but felt it needed investigation.

Eventually they decided to meet at Paddington to catch the 4:15 back to Oxford and then drive on to Stratford. As Kennington wasn't an area cruised by taxis, they phoned for a minicab which dropped Mike at the Museum in Lambeth Road en route for the West End.

He felt a little conspicuous as he walked up the path through a rose garden and a trifle uneasy as he passed under two massive '15-inch' guns from a battleship. Perhaps his unease was caused by a curious feeling, even a suspicion, about the general in the faded photograph. There must be a reference library in the museum, he thought, where Yamashita's military career could be examined. Mike walked up the steps and between the pillars. The officious military air was unlike the relaxed atmosphere of Oxford's academia. Mike expected to be challenged at any moment with, 'Halt who goes there?'

At a turnstile he was searched and as he didn't want to see the exhibits, he was taken to reception and issued with a bright red 'visitors' security pass, which was clipped to his lapel. Then a pretty young woman in a scarlet sweater took him upstairs to the Bookroom high in the dome, where he was handed over to yet another assistant in a red sweater.

'Would it be possible to find out something about a Japanese general called Yamishita?'

'I'm sure we can help; just a moment.' She hurried away to the library shelves and returned thumbing through volume XVII of the World War II Encyclopaedia, 'Here we are, "Tomoyuki Yamashita". Would you like to look at it?'

'Please.' Mike took the book to the circular table in the centre of the room and started to read.

YAMASHITA, Lt. General Tomoyuke (1885-1946). Highly regarded Japanese general, with a considerable reputation as a strategist. Served in the Russo-Japanese War, WWI and Sino-Japanese

War. Military Attache in Berne (1919) and Vienna and Budapest (1927). Led delegation to Berlin (1940) and met Adolph Hitler and Mussolini. At outbreak of War in the Pacific (December 1941), he was given the command of the 25th Army with orders to invade Malaya and Singapore, where he gained the nickname 'The Tiger of Malaya'. With a comparatively small army (30,000) he bluffed and outwitted the Allied forces (100,000) into surrender (15 February 1942). Called to command Japanese forces in the Philippines and charged with their defence. He surrendered 3rd September, 1945 and was hanged for war crimes (23rd February 1946). He has been the subject of controversy ever since.

So, Mike thought, there was a link even though it was a tenuous one between the General and the Philippines. He had been in charge of the archipelago for part of the war. Was that all? Was this single fact the reason for the persistent niggle at the back of his mind? Or was there something else? Mike returned the book and thanked the librarian.

He had a little time before he had to meet Anna at Paddington so decided to head for Hatchard's in Piccadilly and then have a cup of tea in Fortnum's.

He had just passed through the War Museum's main door when a voice behind him called, 'I say, young fella.' It was the tall and erect military figure, the important-looking person he had noticed working in the Bookroom in shirt sleeves and MCC braces. 'Could you spare a moment?'

Mike paused while the man caught up with him.

'D'you have a handkerchief?'

If Mike had thought about it, the request couldn't have been more surprising. 'Sorry?'

'Handkerchief. . . do you have a handkerchief?'

'D'you mean. . ?'

'Has someone given you one?'

'N. . . no.'

'Oh dear. Y. . . you didn't buy one?' He spoke with a clipped nasal accent.

'No.' Mike stood quite still; what could the old buffer be talking about?

'Ah! I can see I need to apologise. Let me introduce myself. Fergus Colerangle's the name. I was on General Sir Arthur Percival's staff in the Far East at the end of the war. At the moment I'm writing the history of my regiment.'

He paused and sniffed before continuing, 'I heard you ask about Yamashita. Y'know he sacked Singapore before taking charge of the Philippines for the Japs. . . Well, it's said he buried a lot of gold from Singapore somewhere in the Philippines before he surrendered. And it's never been found,' he shook his head and sniffed again. 'Some say it's as much as 1,500 tons. And the map showing the gold's whereabouts was drawn on a handkerchief. And these "handkerchiefs" are often sold by con men in the Far East. So I thought you might've bought one.'

'No. . . 1,500 tons of gold?'

'Somethin' like that.' He sniffed; it was clearly an affectation, not a cold. 'It makes the fabulous riches of the Arabian Nights pale into insignificance.'

'It's certainly a lot of gold!'

'About £9 billion.'

'And Yamashita buried it?'

'So they say.'

Mike's mind raced ahead. This must be the connection. The killings in Stratford weren't motivated by drugs, but gold. . . more gold than anyone had ever imagined. Certainly enough gold to be the reason for murder. Was this the link? And somehow Marco Devine was involved? Mike needed to get back to Stratford. He refocused again on the old soldier and heard him saying, 'D'you live in London?'

'No. Sussex.'

'Could we share a cab to Victoria?'

'At the moment I'm staying in Stratford, so I need Paddington, I'm afraid.'

'Ah. . . In that case I'll stay,' He sniffed again. 'And do a little more work. I'm in the middle of a chapter about regimental mascots and I'm findin' it all rather dull. . . Stratford you say? Takes me back to my youth. When I was at Radley, we did a play by that Shakespeare fella. . . Called Coriolanus. Yes, Coriolanus. . . I remember now. . . he was a soldier. His real name was Gaius Martius. . . but they called him Coriolanus after he captured Corioli.' He sniffed again and paused. 'D'y'know. . . Gaius Martius was just like Yamashita. . . he was a soldier. . . a fighter. . . wasn't much good at anything else. Well mustn't keep you, dear boy. Goodbye.'

As he strode away he called over his shoulder, 'Don't touch a "handkerchief" if y'offered one, they're all counterfeits.'

Mike watched Fergus Colerangle vanish back into the Imperial War Museum and then he strode away whistling softly to himself. The tune and the words going through his mind were Cheerio Chin-Chin Goodbyee. His spirits soared; his feet flew as he headed past Lambeth Palace. Once over the bridge he managed to hail a taxi to take him to Paddington. Thoughts of Hatchards and Fortnums fled from his mind; his one aim was to get to Anna and tell her the news. The key. . . the motive. . . the link. . . the connection. . . the reason for the murders, wasn't drugs at all - but gold; astonishing amounts of G O L D.

6: LOVE'S LABOUR'S LOST

'So it's gold. . . that's what it's all about' Anna clasped her hands with excitement as she turned to look out of the window. The train clattered over some points as it raced towards Oxford. Anna had only just caught it, leaving it to the last moment as usual. And she hadn't been able to sit with Mike until Reading, when a group of ladies who had been on a shopping spree in London, vacated their seats amidst a flurry of shopping bags. Once they were seated together, Mike told her about his discoveries at The Imperial War Museum, including the details of Yamashita's gold.

After much rattling and rolling the train returned to its rhythmic and slightly soporific acapella of wheels on rails. It wasn't until a train rushed in the opposite direction with a great whoosh that Anna came back to the present. She turned back to Mike, 'Gold. . . so that's it.'

'Well that's what Fergus Colerangle said.'

'And 1,500 tons?'

'Ah-huh.'

'It must be worth a fortune?'

'More than a king's ransom. . . £9 billion at a rough guess.'

'How do we know he's telling the truth?'

'We don't. But he said that he was on the staff of General Sir Arthur Percival at the end of the war. If he was, then he would certainly know about Yamashita.'

'How does it tie in with Marco?'

'I don't know. . . except that amount of gold would easily tempt a greedy man. And travelling around the world for filming would give Marco the opportunity to smuggle it in his car. The Bugatti must weigh a ton, so a few extra kilos wouldn't be noticed; the gold could even be smuggled as spare parts. It all makes much more sense than drugs.'

'Mmm. . . it does.'

'First thing tomorrow we must see Gillian Wykeham-B and find out where Marco garaged the Bugatti, then search it and the garage thoroughly.'

'What about the "dark lady"?'

'I don't know. At lunch we were both certain it wasn't Emily Lanier.'

'That's what we thought then.'

'You've changed your mind?'

'No. . . but the "dark lady" must fit in somewhere.'

'Where?'

'I don't know. May be we've been looking for the wrong one.'

'How do we look for the right one?'

'Get in touch with Clyde Tombaugh, invite him for a meal and see if he can give us any more names?'

'When d'you have in mind?'

'Any time. . . but not tonight, there's no food at Bull Street.'

'I could take care of that.'

'How?'

'We'll be at Oxford in a few minutes. You 'phone Clyde and ask him if he can come to supper, and I'll dash to the covered market and do the shopping. Then we'll meet back at the car.'

'Are you sure?'

'Absolutely.'

'What time shall I say?'

'Ask him for eight.'

The train began to slow and in the distance, the city of dreaming spires came into view. 'Here we are.' Mike stood and lifted Anna's jacket down together with a shiny red carrier bag.

'I've been shopping,' Anna said rather sheepishly. It was going to take her a long time to get used to spending her husband's hard-earned money on herself.

'So I've noticed — I'm glad.' Mike smiled and did his best to encourage and reassure her.

* * * * * *

After changing, Anna came downstairs a little before 8

o'clock and found Mike busy in the kitchen. 'Am I allowed to see what's cooking?'

'Of course,' Mike looked up and smiled 'It isn't a secret. Let me show you. Then I want to see your new jacket.' He led her to inspect the various dishes in different stages of preparation. 'We're going to start with smoked venison and horseradish.' On the plates were paper-thin slices of venison, garnished with raddichio, fresh basil and a little horseradish.

'Mmm. . . that looks good.'

'To be followed with stir-fried squid, Mange-tout and oyster sauce. I'll cook that at the last moment. Oxford market had some marvellously fresh squid and I've blanched it so it'll cook very quickly — just a matter of seconds. Then we'll finish with cheese and fruit. I got some Brie, ripe figs and prickly pears.'

'I don't know how you do it?'

'It's easy when it's your job,' Mike laughed.

Any further discussion was thwarted by the doorbell, and about an hour and a half later as they settled back to enjoy the cheese the professor said, 'L'me get this straight. . . You've actually found an actress called Lanier, who worked for the RSC? I think that's remarkable.'

'Yes, but there's no way that she's connected to the murders. She's from the Philippines, but apart from that and the fact that she worked here in the theatre, there's no link with Marco. She's a slender wisp of a thing; I can't imagine even her holding a gun, let alone shooting one.'

Anna turned to Clyde Tombaugh, 'I agree. In my mind, it's impossible for her to be the killer.'

The professor shrugged, 'You must be careful when talking about impossibilities. I always remember a headline in the *National Observer* in 1976; the day after Nadia Comaneci got the maximum score at the Olympic Games. It said: "The Impossible Isn't." If you're an academic, you soon learn never to say "impossible," because someone will prove you wrong. Crime isn't my subject, but surely the point about criminals is they don't look like criminals and killers don't look like killers. So what's new?'

'It isn't just her looks,' Anna interjected. 'And it's much more than feminine intuition; it just isn't possible.'

'OK. OK.' Clyde went on the defensive. 'Let's look for something else.'

Mike reached for the small pad near the telephone so that he could make notes.

'If. . .' Clyde Tombaugh took a little more Brie and Mike filled his glass with wine. 'If you want to think seriously about the "dark lady", then you must start with the question of authorship.'

Anna looked up sharply, 'Do we have to go into all that again? You've started to convince Mike, but not me. I can't believe that it was anyone but Shakespeare; It's nonsense to think otherwise. He was born here in Henley Street, and he wrote the plays — everybody knows that.' She sighed, 'Oh Clyde forgive me, but there've been two murders. Surely it's the wrong time for the luxury of academic debate.'

Mike watched his wife vent her feelings and wondered if her problem really was the question of authorship; or was the whole tangled business of the killings something that had caused her too much stress? He even wondered if they should stop the investigations? But he came to the conclusion that he knew her well enough, and was sure that she wouldn't rest until the job was done.

Clyde waited until she had finished and then said quietly, 'Yeah. I know how you feel. Sometimes I don't think its worth it myself. But if you want to know the identity of the "dark lady", you must ask the right questions. If you don't, you'll never get the right answer.'

Anna was still for a moment. Her forehead wrinkled and finally she nodded her head in agreement. 'Yes, of course, you're right.' She struggled for words, 'Do we have any evidence that William Shakespeare, born in Stratford-upon-Avon, didn't write the plays?'

'No, but we don't have evidence that he did. . .'

Anna opened her mouth and raised her hand, but Clyde continued, 'Anna, let me finish. . . We have evidence that Gulielmus Shaksper was born here. . .

well we know that he was christened on 23rd April, 1564. He reappeared occasionally in the history of the town, providing you accept, that Will Shaxspere or Will Shagspere was the same person as Gulielmus Shaksper. But none of those gentlemen or any other with a similar name had any connection with Henley Street. Your Bernard Levin called the birthplace, "one of the biggest frauds in England".'

'But he wrote the plays,' Anna said, almost banging the table with frustration.

'Stratford's Shaksper's parents were illiterate,' the professor exploded. 'His wife was illiterate. Of his two daughters, Judith was illiterate and Susanna, so far as we know, could do no more than write her name.'

'But that's no argument,' said Mike, 'for saying that he didn't write the plays.'

'Sure... but, then how do you explain that there's no reference to him going to school here, that there's no record that he had any literary interest, let alone aspirations. That when he died, he didn't leave any books? Not one book was mentioned in his will, not even a note-book. And, he didn't impress his fellow townsmen with anything worthy of fame. He certainly wasn't known as a writer; the burial register simply says "Will Shakspere, gent". And to add to the mystery, it was nearly seventy years after his death before anyone linked the playwright with Stratford — and that was John Aubrey in *Brief Lives*. The Encylopaedia Britannica says that the acceptance of Stratford as Shakespeare's birthplace didn't take place until the end of the eighteenth century — over 200 years later.'

'Clyde,' said Mike, 'Let's accept what you say for a moment and go on to the next step of trying to identify the "dark lady".'

'OK.' Clyde saw that Mike was ready to make notes. 'Why don't you put on one side of your pad: (i) Shakespeare (ii) Francis Bacon (iii) Edward de Vere. Now next to Shakespeare write, Lucy Negro, Abbess de Cerkenwell, Jacqueline Field, and Emilia Bassano...'

'Lanier.'

'Sure. OK. OK. Emilia Lanier. Then next to Francis

Bacon put Mary Fitton, and next to Edward de Vere write: Anne Vavasor.'

'Vavasor?'

'Yep... Vavasor V-A-V-A-S-O-R... a ravishing beauty from Yorkshire.'

'Any more?'

'No, that's it. That's the complete list of "dark ladies", so far as I know.'

'Thanks.'

'You're welcome.'

Much to Mike's relief, the conversation returned to more general topics and the desert wine continued to flow until the last drop had been enjoyed. Anna made coffee, and blackcurrant tea for their American guest. By the time he was heading down Chapel Street the Guild Chapel clock struck 1 am. As he put his key to the latch of Harvard House, Clyde Tombaugh quietly breathed to himself the old night watchman's cry 'Tis one of the clock and all's well.'

Elsewhere, most of this delightful little Warwickshire town was tucked up safely in bed. A new wave of Kamikaze tourists were asleep in The Prince of Denmark Hotel, their flesh no longer willing and spirits decidely weakened by the rigours of modern travel. Only a handful of kitchen porters was left scouring pots and even fewer diners were making their unsteady way home along Stratford's ancient thoroughfares. In the theatre, wardrobe mistresses had put the last pieces of the linen into the washing machines and the wig girls blocked the final wig for shampooing and setting the next day. Duty managers were making a final tour of the auditoria and dressing rooms, before throwing the last bolt and turning the ultimate key for the night. Outside, a watery moon had risen over the sleeping town. Soon a new day would begin, and the frantic rhythm of life would start all over again.

* * * * * *

'Miss Wykeham-Barnes, please. Hello... Gillian? Yes... fine thank you... We saw her yesterday... I'm sure you're right it can't be her. . . well, we wondered if you could help us with the garage where Marco kept his car? Yep, the Bugatti. . . yes. The Other Place? OK. . . we'll pick up the keys from the foyer. . . and we will return them, I promise you. . . Thanks. . . goodbye.'

When they called for the keys they found they had a label attached bearing the address of one of the older houses at the far end of Southern Lane. The elderly lady who owned the property was a sprightly eighty year old who didn't drive, so she was delighted to augment her income by letting the garage to someone from the Royal Shakespeare Company. The shortage of any form of parking in the town meant that she always had a waiting list, particularly as the garage was so near to the theatre.

Mike and Anna arrived to find that the garage door opened directly onto the street. Mike unlocked and lifted it so that the well balanced door swung up into the roof space. Before them, like a ghost from the past, was Marco Devine's Bugatti — rumoured to have once belonged to Ettore Bugatti himself. From the famous radiator grill and two large headlamps a long sleek bonnet swept back to an open cockpit for the driver. Behind a second windscreen was a covered passenger compartment. Mike and Anna had only seen the car briefly on the night of the shooting; now they stood admiring the classic lines of a Bugatti Royale Coupé Napoleon.

Mike could have stood longer staring at the sheer elegance of the engineering, but Anna's mind was on the task ahead, 'Where do we start?'

'The police have done a very thorough search and forensic tests, so we're just looking for evidence of the gold.'

'Where would they hide it?'

'I'm sure we won't find any,' He pulled a face and jiggled his hand in a *comme ci; comme ca* gesture. 'But if we're lucky we might find some indication that it's been here. There might be the container that it was shipped in, or evidence of smelting.'

'What would that be like?'

'Some sort of crucible. . . big enough for an ingot. . . and something to heat it with. . . a gas appliance. . . or oxy-acetylene equipment.'

They set about their different tasks with Anna looking in the boot and passenger cab while Mike scouted around the rest of the garage. At the far end below a window, a work bench ran the whole length of the wall. On it, a tool cabinet was standing open like a book. It was fitted with everything that a motor mechanic would need, from screwdrivers and spanners to feeler gauges for tappits and distributors.

Mike poked about under the bench and found an old hydraulic jack on wheels, a five-gallon drum of oil and plenty of the normal rubbish that would collect in a garage. He gave a jubilant cry. 'I think I might've found what we're looking for.' He lifted a wooden box about the size of an attache case onto the bench.

Anna came over, 'There's nothing in the car.'

'No I didn't think there would be. I'm sure this is what we want.'

The lid had originally been nailed down, but had been prized opened, and was now held in place with one or two nails gently driven home. Mike took a large screwdriver and levered it open. Whatever it had contained was gone; only a handful of polystyrene packing pebbles remained. He turned the lid over; the crate was addressed to: Peter Warwick, 109 Southern Lane, Stratford-upon-Avon, England. Attached to the lid were the customs and freighting documents, which declared it had come from the Philippines via Heathrow by courtesy of Fastair Cargoes.

Anna stared into the empty box. 'Do you think this was where the gold was?' She picked up some of the packing material; they reminded her of Chinese fortune cookies.

'No. The documents say it was a flywheel.'

'From a car?'

'Presumably a Bugatti, but it isn't here.'

'Maybe it's been fitted to. . . to the engine. . . or whatever?'

'Possibly, but where is the one they took out?'

Anna looked nonplussed.

'Well it certainly isn't here. But under the bench is what I think is a portable furnace.' They stooped to look as Mike dragged it out. They felt that they were getting somewhere at last. A flicker of fresh energy goaded them on.

At that moment a car pulled up outside and hooted; a few moments later Sergeant Percy Williams appeared. 'Hello. Miss Wykeham-Barnes said you'd be here. I've just dropped in to tell you we've arrested a couple of Filipinos.'

'For murder?'

'No.' The sergeant shook his head. 'But they've both been charged with the possession of drugs — cannabis and cocaine. My boss still thinks that drugs are the key to this whole business, and that Marco Devine was tied in somewhere. But we can't work out where at the moment.'

'I think you're wrong,' said Mike determined not to lose his new train of thought or waste the new evidence they had found.

'Now Mr Main, you were very lucky in Brighton; most murders are solved by a lot of boring leg work and sheer persistence. The police'll get there in the end, just you wait and see. And when they do I think you'll find this will've been about drugs.I suppose you think it's got something to do with your brunette?'

'Dark lady,' Anna corrected.

'We do,' Mike explained. 'Shakespeare's "dark lady" was probably called Emilia Lanier, and we've found a girl in London called Emily Lanier. She had a boyfriend called Jimmy Yamashita, and at the end of the war a Japanese general called Yamashita buried a lot of gold in the Philippines. That's what the whole thing is about... gold.'

There was silence for a few moments.

The sergeant sighed, 'Sir, I think I've got to remind you that this is rural Warwickshire; it's not the south coast. Tourists may occasionally loose a handbag, or their credit cards, or even the odd camera. There are cattle thieves about, and there might be a few antiques or the occasional "old master" taken from a country house. And just outside our patch there's Birmingham with all the problems of an inner city. . . joy riding, muggings and drugs. . . but not gold, Sir, not gold.'

'Well, sergeant, we think the murders were about gold, and we're looking for evidence that links them. For instance this crate, it could've been used to bring the gold into the country.'

Pedantically the sergeant inspected the box and the lid, if only to humour Mike. 'Well it says it contained a flywheel, Sir.'

'But it could've been a gold flywheel. That might've been the way they smuggled it into the country. And we've just found this — probably used for smelting.' Mike pointed to the furnace.

'Sir, your average Warwickshire villain doesn't know anything about GLD.'

'GLD?' said Anna.

'Yes. . . Good London Delivery. . . It's the standard size for gold bars today. . . 12.5 Kilos. I learned about that when I was in Brighton. Now that's the place for gold; they'd melt down "rough" gold there any day and turn it into GLD so they could sell it quickly and easily.'

'But where does the "dark lady" fit in?' Anna persisted.

'I don't know. I'm not even sure she does.'

'But that's what Marco said before he died.'

'You think he did. But he'd just been shot; he could've been saying anything.'

'I heard him. I know what he said.' Anna was adamant. 'And I think it's obvious he was talking about Shakespeare's "dark lady".'

'But who was Shakespeare?' said the policeman.

'What do you mean?' asked Anna; she looked at him incredulously.

'I didn't know anything about him when I saw you two days ago, so when I left you I went to the library and borrowed a book called: Shakespeare Scientifically

Surveyed. I don't think I would understand any of his plays, but I understood the book. It sets out to prove that the fellow who lived in Stratford four hundred years ago couldn't've written the plays... D'you know what the average vocabulary is?'

'No.'

'Well, someone who's been educated rarely uses more than 4,000 words. The Old Testament has 5,642 words. A great poet like Milton might use — *might use* 8,000. D'you know how many words Shakespeare used?'

'No.'

'To be precise 17,677. And he was clever, he used 7,200 — that's more than occurs in the whole Bible — only once and never again.' The sergeant was obviously proud of his newly acquired knowledge and determined to flaunt it.

'Is this really helpful?' Mike was beginning to feel that they were wasting their time and should get on with trying to find the killer.

'You're right. I certainly need to get back to work, but I thought you'd like know about the arrests.' The sergeant started to walk towards his car and then turned back. 'The key to this whole thing is drugs, you'll see... goodbye.'

'Goodbye.'

They watched him drive away, then Anna said, 'Well, where does that leave us?'

'Up a creek without a paddle I think, if you want me to put it politely.'

'Shall we take the key back and ask Gillian about Anne Vava... the... er ravishing beauty from Yorkshire?'

'No. I think we should forget it.'

Anna was stunned by this apparent turn-around in Mike's thinking. It stopped her in her tracks.

Mike drew the garage door down, locked it and then continued, 'I think we've been very silly. The odds against finding a Lanier must've been a million to one. and we actually found one; Clyde Tombaugh was amazed at that. The more I think about it, the more I realize that she must be the lady we're looking for.

We've got to go back to London and see her again. And I wouldn't mind popping into the British Library, to see the Promus — or whatever Bacon's manuscript was called.'

They headed back towards the theatre deep in thought. Under his breath Mike was saying, 'It must be Emily Lanier. She's got be the one. . . she's got to be. And it's all to do with gold. . .'

7: THE COMEDY OF ERRORS

The taxi turned into Great Russell Street; on one side was the YMCA which somehow managed to look like a dark towering fortress clinging to the side of a cliff, and on the other the Headquarters of the TUC; an icon of the heady days when labour still used its muscle to bargain for pay and conditions. Even Epstein's figures on the forecourt managed to look slightly dispirited and depressed by the present situation.

By the time the taxi had safely negotiated to the far end of the street, it had left behind the tawdriness of Tottenham Court Road and entered the leafy, scholarly, elegance of Bloomsbury. The whole experience was like a flash-back to the turn of the century, and it was only the street trader in a leather jacket and Gucci shoes, selling 'Egyptian Hieroglyphs on GENUINE papyrus' that marked the scene as belonging to the 1990s.

The taxi pulled up outside the British Museum. Once through the gates, and beyond the iron railings, Mike and Anna walked towards the famous portico. They presumed that they would head straight for the Reading Room beneath the massive beehive dome, but security was much tighter than in Oxford and the Imperial War Museum, so they had to arm themselves with a collection of tickets and passes.

At last they were taken by a lively young West-Indian woman to the manuscript room and initiated into the rites of passage for those who wish to study there. 'These bound volumes,' she declared with a hint of Bajan, 'are the catalogues. Make your request on a ticket;' she then pointed to the little pads below the shelf. 'It normally takes about twenty minutes to get the things you want. No more than six manuscripts may be taken out at any time. And at all times,' she assumed the attitude of a school mistress, 'they must be kept on the book rests, and only pencils used for making notes.'

When they had time to look around, they found that they were in a smallish room. Thirty people were working in the embalmed silence. However, once Mike and Anna had grown used to the atmosphere it was clear that several were conversing in a subdued way as they scrutinized documents ranging from beautifully illuminated gospels to early autographs of English writers.

Mike took down the catalogue volume marked 'BAAB - BORE' and opened it at Sir Francis Bacon. There were at least two pages of listed items, which he scanned for any sign of the *Promus*. As he finished, and not wanting to break the silence, he scribbled a note to Anna: 'I can't see anything remotely like *The Promus*. Can you spot it?'

While Anna searched, Mike consulted the volume 'SARS - STAI' and filled in a ticket to see, 'William Shakespeare verses on his mulbury tree at Stratford — eighteenth-century manuscript.' When it arrived, they both enjoyed sitting and looking at it for a few moments. Eventually Mike suggested that they should go for a coffee and plan the next move.

Having returned the manuscript, they retraced their steps through the Grenville Library, across the main foyer and through the room housing Prehistoric Greece, to the cafe. Soon they were at a table enjoying two steaming cups of coffee.

'I'm not sure what's gone wrong, but I couldn't see anything remotely like the Promus?'

'Nor could I.'

'I suppose scholars might know it by a different name?'

'That's possible. We'll have to check that with Clyde.' Anna stirred her coffee. 'I enjoyed seeing a poem that was actually supposed to be written by Shakespeare and written in Stratford too.'

Mike nodded in agreement, 'Yes, and about the Mulbury Tree.'

'I don't follow?' She looked at him blankly.

'Clyde had a carving knife and fork with wooden handles on his mantlepiece. There's a little brass plate that said they were made from the Mulbury tree that once stood in the garden of New Place.'

'Really?'

'Yes. You must ask to see them the next time we're there.'

Mike paused, 'I've got so caught up with the whole question of authorship that I tend to forget someone actually wrote the plays.' He stopped again and looked into the distance as though remembering something. Finally he added, 'I had a strange thought last night. . .'

'About the plays?'

'No, Shakespeare.'

'Mmm?'

'Well, the more I've looked into the background of the man the more I'm convinced that Mr Shaxspere of Stratford didn't write the plays. I've never thought about it much, but in the back of my mind I've always regarded Shakespeare as an essential part of English history; someone whose existence wasn't even to be questioned; I thought that the pages of history were littered with evidence that pointed to him. On the other hand, I've always been agnostic about Christianity. But since Claire's death, I've become more and more convinced about Christianity, and now I've become agnostic about Shakespeare!' Mike took a drink of coffee. 'I suppose I thought Christianity wasn't real, and now I believe it is, and I thought Shakespeare was real, and now I feel he wasn't. . . it's very strange.' He turned to Anna as though expecting an answer.

She thought for a moment. 'Why do you think we do that with Christianity; not take it seriously, I mean?'

'I suppose if we don't look at it too carefully it can't make too many demands on us.'

'Yes, that's what it must be.'

'So, what's the next move?'

'Cleaver Square?'

* * * * * *

They left the quiet publisher's world of Bloomsbury and

crossed the Thames to the shabbier district of the Elephant and Castle; from there they turned into Kennington Lane and then found Cleaver Square again.

Mike rang the doorbell, and noticed the door was slightly ajar. After a few moments he rang it again, but there was still no response. A telephone started to ring somewhere in the building, but it also went unanswered. Mike pushed the door and it swung open so that the telephone immediately sounded louder and more urgent.

A large oriental jar that had been used for holding umbrellas and walking sticks was smashed and lay on its side; its contents were scattered across the floor.

The telephone stopped ringing, and Mike half stepped inside the house and called out, 'Hello? Anyone here?' And a second time, 'Hello?'

Still no reply. Somehow they sensed that the building was empty, and as if barefooted on a pebble beach they stepped gingerly over the walking sticks and climbed the stairs towards the drawing room on the first floor. Mike led the way. On the landing it was obvious that something was seriously wrong. The suit of armour was on its side and the rest of the drawing room looked as though it had been hit by a storm.

Mike was first to see Emily Laniers's body lying just beyond the sofa. It sprawled awkwardly with the bottom part of her torso twisted in the attitude of a high jumper doing a scissor kick to clear the bar. There must have been a fight; there was plenty of blood everywhere and lying close to the body was one of the Japanese swords with a heavily stained blade. And the place where it should have been hanging on the wall was noticeably empty; the sunlight had bleached its shape onto the wallpaper.

In the instant that it took for him to take in the scene, Mike turned and ushered Anna back towards the door. 'I don't think we should go in there. It's not very nice.'

'What's happened?'

'Emily Lanier has been killed.'

'Where?'

'Beyond the sofa; we'd better go downstairs and call the police.'

They resisted the temptation to tiptoe down the stairs and in the hallway found the 'phone on a small table made out of a portable incense burner. Mike dialled 999 and was quickly put through to the police.

'. . .Yes that's right Cleaver Square. . . no Cleaver C-L-E-A-V-E-R. . . off Kennington Lane. . . yes. . . Michael Main. . . near the pub in the left hand corner.'

They walked outside; somehow it didn't seem right to wait in the house. Anyway neither of them felt strong enough to share a room with another corpse. They were only there a matter of minutes, when an unmarked police car screeched to a halt outside the house. A swarthy young man in jeans and sweatshirt emerged.

'Mr Main?'

'You're the police?'

'That's right, Guv. . . er. . . DC Frank Turner.' He continued chewing a sweet as he showed his warrant card, which he produced from a hip pocket. 'You've found a body?'

'Yes, upstairs in the drawing room, on the first floor.'

They followed him upstairs and in a single glance he took in the scene as though it was an everyday occurrence. 'I think we'd better go back down. I need to use the car radio.'

Back outside by the car, two more police vehicles and an ambulance had arrived, all with flashing blue lights. Some of the patrons of The Prince of Wales and a few curious neighbours from across the square had wandered over to see what was happening. The young policeman in jeans consulted a uniformed officer in one of the cars and then came back to Mike and Anna. 'I need to get a statement. Can we sit in my car? Then we won't get in the way of the team that's about to go into the house.' Once they were seated he took out a notebook, 'You were a friend of the. . . er. . . lady upstairs?'

'No. We've only met her once.'

'Business acquaintance?'

'No.'

83

'Let's start again.' He looked at them rather testily and cleared his throat, 'Name?'

'Main,' said Mike. 'Michael and Anna.'

'Address?'

'Well, we're from Kings Nympton in Sussex. But at the moment we're staying in Stratford on a sort of holiday.'

'I'd better take the address.'

They gave him the details. The young policeman no longer even tried to be gentle. 'How would you describe your relationship with the deceased?'

Anna had been silent since the discovery of Emily Lanier's body. But it was as if the policeman had pressed a button and all emotion of the past few days was released in a torrent. She spoke of their reason for visiting Stratford. That they'd gone there for a few days' break as they both had books to finish, if they were to meet their publishers' deadlines. She related the incident of the shootings. When she stuttered to a halt, the policeman said, 'I'd better try and get all that down.' He uncapped a pen, 'You went to Stratford for a holiday and to do some writing?'

'Yes.'

Once again they told the story of the last few days, occasionally catching each others eyes and watching the young policeman grow more and more intrigued. 'I think I'm beginning to follow,' he said at last.

'That's why we came to see her.'

'You thought she was involved?'

'We weren't sure. But once we got back to Stratford we were; that's why we returned.'

'And now she's dead?'

'Yes.'

'Where does that leave us?'

'I don't know. We'll need to think about that.'

'Mmm. . . and I'll need to take you to the station to sign this. We'll obviously have to get in touch with the Warwickshire police. . .'

'Oh, she had a boyfriend. . .'

'Yeah?'

'Yamashita. . .'

'Yamashita? There was an incident involving that name in Knightsbridge this morning.'

'That could have been her boyfriend. . . Jimmy Yamashita. . . Beauchamp Place. . . it's a gallery.'

'Yeah that's it. Hang on a second.' He got out of the car and talked to the uniformed officer who had just emerged from the front door of the house. He quickly came back, 'The boss says we're to go back to the nick via Knightsbridge to see if there's a link.'

As usual Beauchamp Place was thronging with people and with a police car outside, Gallery Yamashita wasn't too difficult to spot. Mike and Anna followed their policeman out of the car. Even from the street there was no doubt that there was a connection with the house in Cleaver Square. The gallery was simply furnished with a few stunning *objects d'art* and pictures. The bronzes and terracottas were the same quality as those in Kennington. The two drawings that could be seen through the window were Sesshu's, and there was a suit of scale armour that was obviously the companion of the one lying on its side in the drawing room.

The PC on guard greeted their escort. 'What's brought you up West, then Frank?'

'We've got a body in Kennington. It looked like a domestic. But apparently 'er boyfriend was a geezer called "Yamashita" and the boss thought there might be a link.'

'Well. . . yeah our bloke was called Yamashita. I've just 'eard on the blower that he's copt it on the way to the hospital. So I'spose we'd better call him the late Mr Yamashita.'

'What's the MO?'

'Shot. No apparent motive and it'appened in broad daylight. The lady in the shop over there said one moment she saw 'im dusting things and the next'e was was crawling out of the door with blood on 'is shirt.'

The gallery was much the same as the other tiny shops in the area; quality goods were offered without ostentation. There were already three policemen at work inside. A photographer was going about his tasks while two fingerprint women were dusting every surface with metallic powder, hoping that they might yield a clue to the killer.

Frank said, 'Well its not worth going in, even from 'ere it's the same gear as Kennington.' He turned to Mike, 'D'ya know what sort of antiques those are? Are they Japanese. . ?'

Anna answered, 'Yes and very, very, good Japanese.'

'OK. We'd better get back.' Frank started to take his leave from his colleagues. 'There's a possibility that there's a connection with Stratford-upon-Avon. So be warned, we might have work with our country cousins!' He added wryly, 'I hope you can you manage that?' He turned to go, then remembered, 'If the boss wants me, tell 'im we've gone back to the nick to do the statements.'

Yet again Mike and Anna spent two dreary hours while these were typed. It wasn't until they were signed and sealed that they were finally allowed to go.

By this time they had become quite fond of Frank Turner, a great bear of a young policeman who had ferried them to Knightsbridge and then back to Kennington. Once he had relaxed they discovered a sensitive young man beneath a blustery exterior; one who was going through the agonies of a divorce caused by the difficult shifts involved in police work. As he said with great sadness, 'A policeman's lot is not a happy one.'

Eventually Mike and Anna made their way to Paddington where they just missed the 6:15 Intercity to Oxford. As they were left standing watching the departing train, they spotted Clyde Tombaugh walking through the station, apparently having just arrived. They saw each another at precisely the same moment.

'Hi there. You Britishers always complain about British Rail but let me tell you, compared to Amtrack, it's a winner every time.'

'Our train certainly left on time,' said Anna with a sigh.

Mike said, 'We were just about to go for a meal. Why not join us?'

'Thank you, that's very kind. But I'm just off to the Barbican, to see The Comedy of Errors. I'm meeting some friends from Cambridge, Massachusetts and in any case it's my turn to do the entertaining.'

'Well, another time perhaps.' Then Mike added, 'Actually we came up to London to see the Promus, but we couldn't find it. Are you sure it is in the British Library?'

'Positive. It's in the North Library. I don't have a shelf reference with me, but I have it back in Stratford.'

'Ah. . . we were looking in the manuscript room.'

'Well, it should be there too.'

'Under that name?'

'Sure. Heh wait a moment, it may be listed under an English name.'

'Which is?'

'Sometimes it's called "The Storehouse of Formularies and Elegancies".'

'Well we certainly weren't looking for that.'

Anna looked up at Clyde, 'You've really begun to convince Mike about Shakespeare.'

'Oh good! I'm glad he's coming around to the American way of thinking.'

'American?'

'Sure. Walt Whitman said, "I'm firm against Shaksper — I mean the Avon man, the actor." John Greenleaf Whittier said, "Whether Bacon wrote the wonderful plays or not, I am sure the Shaksper man neither did nor could." Mark Twain referred to the people who thought Shakespeare was from Stratford as *Stratfordolators*. I suppose Americans are not inhibited by history; they see the name as an obvious pseudonym.'

'A pseudonym?'

Clyde Tombaugh was either in no hurry to get to the Barbican or simply reluctant to let go of two possible converts to his theories. He continued to exploit Anna's interest, 'Yeah. The first recorded mention of Shakespeare as a dramatist was in 1593 with the publication of the poem *Venus and Adonis*. And the name "Shakespeare" doesn't appear on the title page, but just as part of the dedication.'

'You're saying that "Shakespeare" is a made-up name?'

'Sure. It was so widely regarded as an invention that at first everybody hyphenated it.'

'But why should anybody make it up?' Anna was genuinely mystified.

'Playwrights create names to tell us about their characters, so presumably he was telling us about himself. You've got *Mistress Quickly*, *Doll Tearsheet* and *Mistress Overdone*. Sheridan gave us the classic *Mrs Malaprop*, Jonson gave us *Brayne-Hardie*. There are two kinds of names that are hyphenated in English: family names that combine two names, *Burne-Jones* is a good example. The other sort are manufactured names that denote an action like *Master Starve Lackey*. In other words they are names that are obviously fictitious. "Shake-speare" belongs to that category.'

'I know I'm dim,' said Anna, putting her hand to her brow, 'but what does it mean?'

Mike gave her a quick smile and laughed, 'Don't be so silly my darling.'

Clyde continued, 'Well it's the most appropriate name for a writer of plays. It would have been too much of a coincidence if the greatest dramatist of our civilization had been born with the name "Shakespeare". "Hasti-vibrans" or "the spear-shaker" was the sobriquet of Pallas Athena, who was said to have sprung from the brow of Zeus brandishing a spear. Pallas Athena was the patron goddess of Athens, home of the theatre. A collection of Shakespeare's poems in 1640 speaks of "the spear of Pallas" shaking and Robert Greene referred to him once as, "Shake-scene".'

'Shake-scene?'

'Yes. . . Heh, you must excuse me, I must be off.' The American paused and then added, 'But if you just want to see a copy of the Storehouse of Formularies and Elegancies — I got one, call anytime tomorrow.'

'Thanks. . . we might do that. What are you seeing tonight?'

'The Comedy of Errors. D'you know some of the other titles that Shakespeare tried for that play?'

'No.'

'Well one was: *The Twins or Which is Which*, and in another production he called it: *Tis All a Mistake.*' Clyde laughed, 'Once or twice I've thought of calling my book on the authorship of Shakespeare: *Tis All a Mistake*. How about that? Now I really must fly. 'Bye.'

They watched him hurrying off. Mike broke the silence, 'Let's go and get something to eat and cheer ourselves up. Why don't we go to Langan's and have their spinach souffle with anchovy sauce?'

'Mmm. . . you're beginning to make me hungry.'

They headed towards the tube; then Mike came to a sudden stop, 'I've just realized. . .'

'What?'

'Well, unless Clyde Tombaugh is behind all this, the only person who knew we were going to see Emily Lanier was Gloria Glasspole. She was with him the night when we met near the Pizza Hut.'

'That's right.'

'So could Gloria Glasspole be the "dark lady" after all?'

8: A MIDSUMMER NIGHT'S DREAM

Midsummer was approaching and the gardens of Stratford were alight with the gentle colours of an English summer; the hedges had become homes and nurseries for whole families of tiny birds. There were no hedges, of course, in the gardens behind Bull Street; there the tiny plots of land were divided by brick walls into precise rectangles. Victorian England not only decreed that every workman should have his home, but a garden too. The only problem being that the same walls that provided privacy also blocked out the sunlight.

Behind 41a, a thick shrub was home for five lusty young sparrows. The slightest movement made them think that food had arrived. They would shoot upright like tiny quivering flames, embryonic wings fluttering, tiny scraggly necks erect and their orange mouths wide open, like a posy of flowers with bright petals seeking the sun.

Near the lintel of the outhouse at the bottom of the garden was a wren's nest; it was no more than a dark hole filled with baby wrens. One had tumbled out onto the brick area in front of the door and lay pathetically on its back with legs crossed over a huge blue stomach, its disproportionately large eyes closed for ever. A flock of young starlings swept into the garden like a group of noisy youngsters alighting from a school bus.

The municipal garden, between the theatre and Clopton Bridge, was a vivid sea of colour; red geraniums, yellow and burgundy wallflowers, golden irises and scarlet and white busy lizzies. Hollyhocks stood as sentries guarding the borders.

If you had stopped to look, you would have found that the most fascinating creatures in the gardens were the caterpillars among the mullein plants. At just the right moment the cocoon seemed to know when the leaves of the shrub were starting to thicken, and a moth would emerge to lay its eggs on the downy surfaces. By now the mullein stood tall and luscious, and the caterpillars were feasting on the rich foliage; they were as beautiful as the plant, with black and yellow markings covering their delicate blue bodies. In two days they would double in size, and then withdraw leaving the leaves fretted with holes and sugared with excrement. Their brief span of life over, they would pull the dark underside of the leaves around them to become invisible. The mullein would have served its purpose for another year.

Bees were everywhere and the world hummed with summer.

* * * * * *

The morning was already warm when Mike and Anna walked to the Prince of Denmark Hotel in Chapel Street. They were shown up to Gloria Glasspole's suite on the first floor. It consisted of a sitting room and two bedrooms, one of which was used as a dressing room by the actress. The sitting room reflected the town and was bright with herbaceous colours; many of Gloria's friends had sent flowers with a 'break a leg' message for the International Season.

Her dresser opened the door, seated them and served coffee, before Gloria swept in looking very much the Hollywood star, in Western boots, white jeans and a revealing silk shirt.

'Yeah, I remember you. We met the other evening outside the Pizza Hut, and you were very sweet to me after the shooting in the shopping mall.'

'Yes,' said Anna. 'And somehow when we got back I found I was still holding your scarf.'

'And you gave it to that nice policeman to return to me. Thank you.' The actress raised her hands in an open gesture, 'So what can I do for you?'

'Well. . .' Mike wasn't sure how to begin. 'Before Marco died, he said the "dark lady".'

'Sure. . . I know that. . . Clyde Tombaugh told me.'

'We think he was probably trying to tell us the

identity of the killer,' Mike paused and the silence was almost audible.

'C'mon baby!' the actress exploded. 'They don't come much darker than me. So what are you getting at?' She calmed down a bit and shrugged, then pulled a face that in a strange way made her look even more attractive. 'He shot at me too. . . remember?'

'Someone shot at you,' Mike wiped his lips with the back of his hand. 'But when we spoke the other night outside the Pizza Hut, we said we were going to see Emily Lanier. Then yesterday in London. . .' Mike fingered his mouth again, 'She and her boyfriend were killed.'

'Oh God no!' Gloria Glasspole went pale and her mouth dropped open. She looked devastated.

But the identical thought crossed Mike's and Anna's minds at the same moment, they were dealing with a star, someone who made their living out of being able to portray every human emotion on the screen; how would they know when she wasn't acting?

'Well, she's dead all right,' said Mike tersely. 'At her boyfriend's flat in Kennington, and he at his gallery in Knightsbridge. They were both brutal killings.'

Gloria dropped her head into her hands for a moment and then looked up. 'OK. . . OK. . . How can I help?'

'What did you do yesterday?'

'As You Like It.'

'During the day? Did you have a matinee?'

'No. We should've been doing Macbeth, but it was cancelled because of Marco's death.'

'Did you go to London?'

'Do I have to answer that?'

'Of course not, but the police might come and ask the same question and then you'd have no choice.'

The room was silent for a few moments. 'Yeah. OK, I went to London. . . so what?'

'What did you do?'

'Saw my son.'

'I didn't know you were married.'

Gloria laughed, 'I'm not.'

'So he's not called Glasspole?'

'No. Why do you ask?'

'I just wondered.'

Gloria sighed. 'Look, I was born in Kingston, Jamaica. Names don't mean much in a ghetto. I've always been called Gloria, 'cos my Ma said I was born on a glorious day. I got my first big break in pictures when they came to Jamaica to film some location shots for a James Bond movie. They liked what they saw, so they gave me a contract. I had to have a new name; in those days Florizel Glasspole was the mayor of Kingston, so I called myself Gloria Glasspole — GeeGee to my friends.'

'Can you prove where you were in London?'

'Can you prove that I wasn't?' She shook her head and raised a hand. 'Look... look, I'm sorry. I just want to get on with my job... OK? I don't want to get involved in your murders. D'ja think I tried to kill myself in the shopping mall?'

Mike didn't stop to answer, 'Marco's background was similar to yours. Have you ever thought about that?'

'Yeah, we talked about it sometime.'

'Did you know him well?'

'How well does anyone know anyone else?'

'Did he have a room here at the Prince of Denmark?'

'Sure... but he never used it. He liked his privacy so he could come and go with his lady friends.'

'Where did he stay?'

'On his er... thing... you know?'

'Thing?'

'Yeah on one of those... slim... thin things... a boat.'

'A narrow boat?'

'Sure a canal boat. It's moored right next to the theatre. Look, I didn't kill Marco.'

There was another pause. Then Mike said, 'Well we'll have to accept what you say. It was kind of you to see us; thanks.' And they stood up ready to go.

* * * * * *

Mike and Anna had already planned to take their lunch on the river, so they walked back to the dairy, opposite

Councillor Norris's office, bought a pic-nic and then hired a boat from the boat-house over Clopton Bridge, near the Swan's Nest Hotel. Mike didn't row far, only until he was opposite the theatre and then he let the boat drift against the bank. They both lay back enjoying the warmth of the sun, and lulled by the gentle murmur of the river gazed up at the blue sky festooned with huge clouds that seemed to have come straight out of a Renaissance painting. Anna was the first to break the silence and said dreamily, 'A penny for your thoughts?'

'Oh I was thinking about summer and how strange it is that midsummer's day comes only three days after the end of spring, and. . .'

'. . .And?'

'. . .And I'm beginning to think there is something magical about this place.' Mike sat up and pointed. 'Look! It's only an old muddy, English river bank — and yet I want to say: "I know a bank where the wild thyme blows, Where oxlips and nodding violet grows. Quite over-canopied with luscious woodbine. . .".'

Anna chuckled, 'You're right, Stratford is magical. I don't have any problems with the idea that a great writer was born here. If you can't write here, in these idyllic surroundings, then you shouldn't be able to do it anywhere.' She paused, 'How about some lunch?'

'What a good idea.'

Soon they were tearing a fresh baguette into chunks, spreading them with great lumps of gooey Brie washed down with *Gran Reserva, CHIVITE*, from Navarra. They had to drink it straight from the bottle because although Mike had remembered to pocket a corkscrew he had forgotten to bring any glasses.

Very quickly they were surrounded by swans and a whole host of tiny ducks, all squabbling their demands for food. They were only driven away by a canal boat, which swung out of the lock in a wide arc, forcing them to move with great reluctance and much flapping of wings and paddling of feet. As the narrow boat passed Mike said, 'Aren't they astonishing? I hadn't realized that they were so brightly coloured. I gather you can hire them for a holiday. Would you like that?'

'No thanks. I like my creature comforts too much. But I wouldn't mind seeing what they're like inside. I wonder if there's much room?'

'Well,' Mike corked the wine and put it back into the bag that had held the bread and the cheese, 'That must be Marco's boat over there by the theatre. We could row over and take a look.'

Anna sat up and looked across the river, 'Where?'

'There,' Mike pointed.

'Are you sure that's his?

'Gloria Glasspole said it was, and it's the only one.'

Anna was still uncertain, 'Are you sure?'

'Even more now... look at its name?'

'*La Belle Noire.*' Goodness! That could be Marco's "dark lady"!'

The design of the narrow boat is peculiar to England and it is sometimes called a 'Monkey boat' after Thomas Monk who invented it. They differ in size, but are all roughly 70 feet long with a 7-foot beam and carry up to 35 tons of cargo. Their decoration has become an art form; a mixture of gaudy colours and a stylized way of representing castles and roses.

Mike stowed the oars as they came alongside the stern of Marco's boat, which had all the marks of being built in the Braunston yard of Nurse Brothers. The shape of the stern showed her to be a Butty boat, one lacking an engine. The power of a narrow boat's engine enables her to pull a Butty boat, allowing twice the amount of cargo to be moved and so doubling the profits of a journey.

Mike looked up at the theatre, where Gillian could just be seen working in her office. Cupping his hands, he called, '*Gill... le... ian!*'

She looked down towards them.

'Can we look at Marco's boat?'

She signalled that she couldn't hear what he was saying.

So Mike tried again, gesturing that they wanted to look at the boat. Gillian waved her permission and with signs demonstrated it was unlocked.

They clambered on board and secured their boat's painter to the towing-pin on the canal boat's stern. Standing directly in front of them in the space normally occupied by the helmsman was the cratch; the gable end of the deck housing which ran the whole length of the boat and covered both the cabin and cargo.

The two doors of the cratch opened outwards and were covered with a brightly painted picture of a castle surrounded with a border of rose buds. When home is limited to the cramped conditions of a barge it must be essential to dream of castles and rose gardens, Anna thought as she glanced briefly at the painting. Mike opened the doors, and they went below. The height of the deck housing was deceptive; standing on the cabin floor, they were surprised at the spaciousness inside. The cabin was furnished as a galley and fitted with everything a cook would need.

Mike opened the back door which would normally lead into the cargo area, but instead they stepped into a sitting room lined with bookshelves. There were several easy chairs, a table covered with photographs of Marco with a number of beautiful women, a TV and a caste-iron wood burning stove. At the far end was a door leading into a bedroom, with a bathroom beyond that. The light was provided by windows let into the side panels of the deck housing.

They walked through the boat in silence, amazed at the luxury hidden away in what appeared to be a very ordinary narrow boat.

'I think we ought to do a quick search,' Mike said.

'What're we looking for?'

'Oh the same as in the Bugatti's garage. . . anything connected with gold.'

They went back through the boat, looking in the cupboards. Although the boat appeared to be lived in, there were clothes hanging in the wardrobes, but there was little else. There was plenty to drink, but very little food; obviously Marco didn't do much cooking, if any at all.

Three cardboard crates of mineral water stacked in a cupboard in the galley were the only thing that caught their attention. It was an unknown brand. The bottles were amber, with orange parchment labels declaring, 'EAU de COLOGNE — *Germany's famous mineral water*'.

'That's a new one,' was Mikes' only comment.

Outside, someone called, 'Ahoy, anyone on board?'

They went back through the cratch and found Sergeant Williams and Gillian Wykeham-Barnes standing on the walkway above them. Gillian greeted them. 'I told the sergeant you were on the boat.'

'Yes,' said the sergeant looking rather tetchy. 'I've only just discovered that Marco had a boat. Up to now, our information was that he was staying at the Prince of Denmark. But apparently all the stuff there belonged to Peter Warwick.'

'Have you seen the name of the boat?' queried Mike.

'No,' unsurprisingly the sergeant's temper made him rather laconic.

'It's *La Belle Noire* so it could be Marco's "dark lady",' said Anna.

'How silly,' said Gillian. 'I should've known that, but you can't see the name from the office, and everybody just calls it "Marco's boat".'

Anna continued talking to the sergeant, 'We've searched it for anything to do with gold.'

'Gold?' echoed Gillian.

'Yes,' Anna turned to her. 'We think that Marco's death was connected with gold smuggling. We've discovered that Emily Lanier's boyfriend was called Yamashita, and his father was a Japanese General who buried a lot of gold in the Phillipines, which. . .'

'Thank you, miss,' the sergeant broke in abruptly 'We are fairly sure that the murders are connected with drugs, and we're targeting our enquiry accordingly.'

'But what about yesterday?'

'All that happened in London served to confirm our suspicion; the Met discovered some white powder at the flat in Kennington, which we believe the toxicologist will. . .'

'That's ridiculous,' said Mike. 'What about the stuff in the Bugatti's garage?'

'We haven't had a report from forensics yet. Incidentally I need to talk to both of you privately.'

'Listen,' said Gillian, 'I'm on my way to a meeting at The Other Place so use my office. The door's unlocked.'

'May we?' Percy Williams' eyes softened as he smiled.

They walked up the stairs at the back of the theatre in silence, with Mike and Anna wondering why the police should suddenly want to see them again. Once in the administrator's office the sergeant said, 'I didn't want to say it publicly, but chief inspector Good wasn't too happy about you two nosing around.'

'Why's that? We helped you solve the case in Brighton,' Mike protested. 'Remember?'

'I explained that, but he wasn't impressed. I think the real problem is the Met; they didn't like your involvement in London yesterday, and one of their senior men phoned Mr Good this morning.' The sergeant breathed in and exhaled noisily, 'The Met like to think that they're the only real policemen and the rest of us are just a bunch of amateurs.'

'But, if it wasn't for us the Metropolitan Police wouldn't know of the connection between Emily Lanier and Marco,' said Anna indignantly.

'Yes, madam, but. . .'

'. . .And they didn't know that the two killings in London were connected until we told them.' Anna's mind raced over the events of yesterday. 'Nor would they've known about Yamashita's buried treasure, so they knew nothing about the gold.'

'Drugs, miss. . .'

'Sergeant, We think you're wrong.' Mike spoke with great firmness.

But the policeman was firmer. 'Sir, we can't stop your research into the authorship of the plays — "the dark lady", etcetera. . . etcetera, but we must insist that you don't get involved in police business.'

There was silence for a few moments. Mike turned and looked out across the river to the spot where they'd recently had lunch. He turned back to the sergeant, 'You're right of course, we shouldn't've got involved.'

'Thank you, sir. Now there is another matter.'

'Yes?'

'Well, it really concerns Mrs Main.' He took a

notebook out of his breast pocket and flicked it open.

Anna had followed Mike's gaze as he had looked out of the window and was lost in a day dream, which had started on a muddy river bank and ended on one 'Where the wild thyme blows'. She heard her name and it brought her out of her reverie, 'Sorry?'

The sergeant rose up and down on his toes. 'You remember Miss Glasspole's scarf?'

'How could I forget?'

'I returned it to her...'

'...She told us.'

'It was badly bloodstained?'

'Yes.' Anna looked puzzled.

'Did it touch anything else... the... er blood I mean?'

'Just the programme I was carrying. I wiped it off, but it stained it a bit.'

'Do you still have it?'

'Yes.'

'Would it be possible to borrow it for a little while?'

'Of course.'

'I'll send a man around this afternoon to get it. Will you be at home.'

'I'm sure we will.'

With the questioning over, they retraced their steps down the staircase and at the bottom said their goodbyes. The sergeant headed back to the police station, and Mike and Anna went to the river side to retrieve their boat. They clambered down into the helmsman's area of the narrow boat, and while Anna untied the painter of their rowing boat, Mike slipped through the cratch and returned holding a bottle of Eau de Cologne.

'I'll tell Gillian I've pinched it.'

They returned the boat to the boat-house and then ambled back through Stratford to Bull Street.

'I don't know about Midsummer's day, but I think I'm suffering from midsummer madness.' Mike dodged a tourist and kicked an empty cigarette packet into the road.

'Why do you say that?'

'Well, it is madness... four killings... a dark lady...

and bottles of mineral water. . . and we aren't any further on than we were three days ago.'

'And officially we've been told not to get involved.'

'Ah!' Mike raised a finger. 'We're allowed: "Shakespearian research," that's what the sergeant said and as I'm convinced that the murders have got something to do with Shakespeare's "dark lady" and Stratford-upon-Avon, I'd think that gives us plenty of leeway. Why d'you think the sergeant wanted a sample of La Belle Noire's blood?'

'Can't imagine.'

They had reached the door of 41a Bull Street. Mike inserted a key and unlocked it. As the door swung open, he leant on the lintel, '*I know a bank where the wild thyme blows.*'

'Really?' Anna pretended surprise. 'Is it the one "*Where oxlips and the nodding violet grow*"?'

'The very same.' He kissed her gently. 'I think there's a comfortable bed upstairs.'

'Now that's the sort of midsummer madness I could enjoy.'

'Me too.'

With that they closed the door and went up stairs.

9: MUCH ADO ABOUT NOTHING

Before marrying, Anna had taught history of art at Roedean the grey Colditz-like building that stands aloof, high on the Downs above Brighton's marina. In the late 1980s she had exchanged with a member of staff of St Paul's Concord, in New Hampshire. It was there she learnt that if Americans were Anglophiles, they were inclined to be more English than the English.

Anna's term in America was during the fall, when New England sports herself in the most stunning autumnal colours. If she had ventured out of 'Scudder,' the school's guest house, anywhere near 4 o'clock in the afternoon she always found herself invited to sit by a roaring fire to enjoy Gentlemen's Relish on toast and Earl Grey tea from a silver teapot poured by someone in baggy cords and a threadbare tweed jacket. In the background the hi-fi invariably played something baroque and the greater part of the bookshelves would be given over to A.A. Milne, C.S. Lewis, J.R.R. Tolkien, Kenneth Grahame, and Jane Austen. And there could well have been a complete set of Beatrix Potter there too.

This all flooded back into Anna's mind as she sat with Mike in Clyde Tombaugh's sitting room on the first floor of Harvard House.

Much paper has been spoiled, to use Dr Johnson's phrase, in trying to understand why so many Americans are fond of England. Having reflected on it, Anna didn't give it a second thought, but took the cup of coffee offered by Clyde, and simply regarded him as a charming example of an American Anglophile. He poured herb tea for himself and it was then that Anna realized that the only really unEnglish thing about him was the way he pronounced 'herb.' He did it in a way that made him sound like a Frenchman.

Once they were seated enjoying their coffee, Clyde picked up a book from the low table next to his chair. 'Well, here it is.' He passed it to Mike.

Mike turned it over so he could read the spine, '*Bacon is Shakespeare*, Sir Edwin Durning-Lawrence, Bt,' he read with surprise.

'Yeah, but it also includes a translation of the *Promus*. That's what you wanted; it's the second part of the book.'

Mike looked at the title page and read, ' "*Bacon's* Promus *of Formularies and Elegancies.*" What an amazing title!'

'Isn't it just?'

Mike flicked through the pages until he found what he wanted and was immediately lost in thought. After a few moments he looked up. 'May I borrow it for a few days?'

'Sure.' Clyde chuckled, 'Anything to help research.' He picked up his cup and lifted it towards his mouth; 'Especially if it confirms my own thinking on the subject.'

Mike was already lost in Sir Edwin's tome.

Anna turned to Clyde. 'You know I'm not convinced. I've been wondering,' she paused. 'Are you sure that there's no record of Shakespeare's life between the time of. . . er. . . say his marriage and. . . his appearance in London?'

Clyde put his hand to his forehead, 'Well. . .'

'Clyde. . . I need your help.' There was a note of frustration in Anna's voice. 'Forget all the stuff about the "dark lady." Is there anything, anywhere, that I can look at which might throw some light on the Stratford man. . . "Shakespeare", "Shaxspere", or "Shagsper". . . whatever you care to call him?'

There was a pause. 'Clyde, help me, please. You're supposed to be the scholar. . . there must be something, somewhere?'

'Well. . . yeah. There is a document that might help. It's called William Shakeshafte, and it's by a man called. . .' He struggled to remember and pulled a face as he looked at the ceiling.

'Its by. . . Chambers. . . Yeah, that's it. . . Chambers. . . E.K. Chambers.'

'Published?'

'1930s... 1940s.'

'Isn't there anything later?'

'Well, you could ask Mary Black at The Shakespeare Centre; she's the archivist of the Royal Shakespeare Company.'

'I might do that.'

Mike hadn't heard any of the last part of the conversation and suddenly put his book down. 'I'm sorry, I'm being rather rude Forgive me, but I'm fascinated by this.'

'We're aware of that, my darling.' Anna had a slightly pained look.

'Clyde.' Mike looked up as he remembered something that he had wanted to say. 'We've found another "dark lady".'

'Another actress?'

'No, it's a narrow boat. It belonged to Marco Devine, and it's moored next to the theatre. It's called *La Belle Noire.*'

'D'you think that's what he was was referring to when he died?'

'I'm not sure. It's probably just a coincidence. We've searched it pretty thoroughly, but it's as clean as whistle.'

'Well...' Clyde looked thoughtful, 'if the "dark lady" was a clue — and *La Belle Noire* is another, then it all points to Gloria Glasspole. She's the only "black beauty" in Stratford at the moment.'

'Yep, but she was shot... which doesn't make sense.' Mike shook his head. 'On the other hand, she was with you when we met by the Pizza Hut, so she knew we were going to see Emily Lanier. She could've got there first and killed her. When we spoke to her just now, she admitted she was in London.'

'*Did* she,' Clyde Tombaugh looked at Mike intensely.

'Y'know I think you should take another look at *La Belle Noire... Gloria Glasspole...* whatever you want to call her.'

Mike stood, 'OK. Thanks for the coffee and for the book. I'm going straight back to devour it. You've given me a lot to think about.'

They stood and shook hands, and Clyde showed them downstairs.

As they stepped into the High Street it was, as usual, teeming with tourists from every part of the world.

'Are you really going back to read?'

'Is that OK?'

'Fine. I need to do one or two things; can we meet at Bull Street for lunch?'

'Let's do that. Get a baguette and I'll prepare something for lunch.'

Anna headed for the Shakespeare centre in Henley Street, opened in 1964 to celebrate the 400th anniversary of the poet's birth.

As she walked into the building a series of glass engravings of Shakespearian characters caught her attention along with a commanding bronze of the bard by John Hutton. She could imagine scholars and academics working in the reading room, especially those who were not as fortunate as Clyde Tombaugh in having Harvard House for their use.

'I'm looking for a document called *William Shakeshafte*. Do you have it by any chance?' Anna addressed the archivist in her office.

'Yes. By E.K. Chambers its in his *Shakespearean Gleanings*.'

'That's it.'

'Can I ask what you're looking for? Are you interested in "the lost years" or "Shakeshafte?" We've got quite a bit of material on both subjects.'

'On Shakeshafte?'

'Yes. In the records of Snitterfield Manor. The poet's grandfather Richard, occasionally called himself "Shakstaff" or "Shakeshafte", as well as "Shakspere." And people think that William might have done the same, especially in the early years'

'Is there any evidence for that?'

'Well. Ben Jonson said Shakespeare had "Little Latin and less Greek," but he understood Latin pretty well, because in his younger years he was a schoolmaster in the country. That's when he could've called himself "Shakeshafte".'

'Ben Jonson?' Anna took a jotter from her handbag.

'Well actually it was John Aubrey, quoting Jonson.

Aubrey was a great collector of biographical gossip.'

'D'we know if Shakespeare was a schoolmaster anywhere? That's really what I'm looking for.'

'There's a possibility.'

'Where would I find something on that?'

'Try the will of Alexander Hoghton. He died in 1581 leaving his servants a year's pay, plus annuities for four players. . . actors. . . one of whom was William Shakeshafte. If he *was* the poet, it's possible he was also "tutor" to the children of Alexander Hoghton and Sir Thomas Hesketh.'

'I don't quite understand.' Anna frowned as she tried to follow.

'Sir Thomas and Alexander Hoghton were close friends and lived near each other. In his will Alexander Hoghton said he hoped his brother would employ the actors, but if he didn't, he wanted Sir Thomas Hesketh to take care of them. . .'

'Where did they live, the Hogtons and the Heskeths?'

'Lancashire.'

'Lancashire? Is it possible to connect Shakespeare with the north-west of England?'

'That's the difficulty.'

'This is the sort of stuff I'm looking for. Where would I find details of the Hoghton will?'

'We've got several books dealing with it. If you'd like to come back tomorrow, I'll have them out for you.'

'That's very kind. Thank you,' said Anna. 'You've answered so many questions. I wish I'd come here sooner.' She paused, 'Could I ask just one more thing?'

'Of course.'

'Do you think Shakespeare. . . the Stratford man. . . wrote the plays?'

'I don't think there's any doubt about it.'

'Well, I've met someone recently called Professor Tombaugh. . .'

'Clyde Tombaugh is a charmer; all the ladies fall for him, so be careful. He's also an academic, and one thing that's true of that breed is that they believe their own theories. . . which can be very dangerous. But the burden of proof is that the plays were written by

William Shakespeare of Stratford.' Mary Black picked up some papers from her desk and laughed as she got up and walked away, 'As soon as anyone proves otherwise we'll have to shut up shop — and so will most of Stratford. Fortunately they haven't done that yet and we still have our jobs.'

Now Anna was lost in thought. Her mind was racing. 'Why didn't I think of asking a woman before?' She said to herself, and then with a new lightness in her step she strode out of the Centre and walked slap-bang into Gillian Wykeham-Barnes.

'Gillian?'

'Hello. How are you?'

'Fine. Thanks for letting us look over Marco's boat yesterday.'

'That's OK. I really should've known what it was called. So forgive me for not knowing it was *La Belle Noire*.'

'That's OK.'

'Did you find anything helpful on the boat?'

'No. Not really. Except. . .'

'. . .Yes?'

'Mike took a bottle of water.'

'*Water*? That doesn't sound like Mike, to me.'

'Mmm. . . he thinks there's something wrong with it.'

'Really?'

'That's what he said.'

'What sort of thing?'

'I don't think he knows.'

'*Water!*'

'Yes it was in a cupboard in the galley. . . there were three cases of a German mineral water called — *Eau de Cologne* would you believe?'

'Oh, those.' Gillian paused briefly and then added, 'Would you like to go to the theatre this evening?'

'Love to.'

'I've got some returned tickets. One of our sponsors has another pressing engagement. They're officially booked out, so you might as well have them.'

'Thank you, that's very kind.'

'Not at all. It's Much Ado About Nothing. They'll be at

the box office... you're getting used to that by now. I'll probably see you tonight. 'Bye.'

' 'Bye.'

When Anna arrived back at Bull Street, Mike was just showing sergeant Percy Williams out. 'Ah, darling, there you are. The Metropolitan Police want to see you.'

'Me?'

'Yes.'

'Sorry, Miss... Mrs Main. They wouldn't take my word for it. They think you know too much about Japanese antiques. It's made them suspicious. So they want to come and see you.'

'Well...'

'Darling, I tried to explain...'

'I'm afraid you've got to see them, Mrs Main; they're insisting. I tried to explain about the restaurant. But, that made them even more suspicious...'

'Apparently,' Mike interrupted with a laugh, 'when the sergeant told them about The Old Nail Shot, they said that they regard restaurateurs with more suspicion than antique dealers!'

'That's right, Miss.' The sergeant nodded sagely and went bright red with embarrassment. 'I told them that yours was a real restaurant... but they didn't seem to understand...'

'And I thought my Michelin star had some value,' said Mike indignantly.

'I'd better see them, I suppose,' Anna sighed.

'Could you say when, miss?' The sergeant was ready to scribble down her reply.

'Tomorrow?'

'What time?' He waited to make a note.

'First thing in the afternoon... say 2 o'clock.'

'Thanks. I'll phone London and let them know,' Percy Williams put his notebook away, said goodbye, got into his car and drove off.

Mike and Anna watched him until he waved as he turned into Chestnut Walk. Back in the house, they made their way to the kitchen, where Mike had begun to prepare lunch.

Within two or three minutes, certainly in no more

than five, it was on the table. All Mike did was to fry some chicken livers which he had already prepared, and toss them in a *mesclum*, a salad of lettuce, *mache* (lamb's tongue) and herbs. He added a little vinaigrette of balsamic vinegar and carried it to the table to be enjoyed with the baguette which Anna had brought back.

Soon they were discussing the discoveries that they had made in the past hour. Mike was full of Bacon's *Storehouse of Formularies and Elegancies*.

Anna speared a morsel of liver and a piece of oakleaf lettuce. 'You think it's authentic?'

'I do.'

'The dates Clyde mentioned. . . of the plays and quotations. . . are they as he said. . . *later* than the *Promus*?'

'They appear to be. I've got to get a copy of *The Complete Works* from Waterstone's. Then I'll be able to confirm it. At the moment the *Promus* seems to be genuine, and so what Clyde said was evidently true.'

Trying to be as casual as possible Anna said, 'I went to the Shakespeare Centre.'

'Interesting?'

'Very. It's that modern building in Henley Street. I did a little research too. There's a chance that Shakespeare was a school master in Lancashire before he became a playwright.'

'Shakespeare?'

'Well, actually someone called William Shakeshafte.'

'There's evidence?'

"Mary Black, the RSC's archivist, is getting it for me. William Shakeshafte is mentioned in the will of Alexander Hoghton, who died in 1581. Shakeshafte worked for him as an actor and probably taught his children at the same time.'

'Shakespeare. . . Shakeshafte. . . there's quite a bit of difference. . . it probably wasn't the same person.'

'According to the records in Snitterfield Manor, William Shakespeare's grandfather sometimes called himself "Shakstaff" and "Shakeshafte" as well as "Shakespeare".'

'Mmm, did he?'

'Uh-hah.'

'But you'll still have to link him with Lancashire?'

'That's what I'm going to work on while you get excited about the *Promus*. And you never know, I might come up with a "dark lady," a sort of Donald McGill Blackpool belle of the sixteenth century. Young Mr Shakespeare's first love. . .'

'That's not possible.'

'Why not?'

'Well,' Mike spoke with a hint of irritation, 'we know all the likely candidates for the "dark lady"; there aren't any more.'

'But people don't know *much* about Shakespeare — that's what we're discovering. A.L. Rowse's theory presumes that the sonnets were autobiographical and that Shakespeare's love affair was a contemporary one. But he could've been thinking about the girl of his dreams, the one he met in Lancashire when he was a young teacher?'

'You'll never be able to confirm it?'

'No, may be not, but I'm going to try.'

They had finished lunch, and Mike leant across the table and took Anna's hand, 'I'm sorry. I'm being very irritable. I think it's because we're not getting anywhere in our search for the "dark lady". He lifted her hand and kissed it. 'What are you going to do this afternoon?'

Half-teasingly Anna replied, 'Try to figure out a way of finding if Shakespeare had any connection with Lancashire.'

'How?'

'I don't know. And you?'

'Finish reading the *Promus* then pop out to get a copy of *The Complete Works* to check the dates. Then plan our next move.'

Anna got up and started to clear the table. 'I nearly forgot. . .'

Mike looked up.

'I met Gillian this morning. She's given us some tickets for tonight. I said we'd love to go.'

'Marvellous. What is it?'

'Much Ado About Nothing.'

'Why don't we have an early meal at Sir Toby's. They open early, so we could eat before the theatre. Then we won't have to think about food.'

* * * * * *

Later that afternoon Anna found herself wandering aimlessly around Stratford-upon-Avon trying to think of a way to link Shakespeare with Lancashire. At one point she found herself staring into the window of a jewellery shop in Henley Street, where there was a display of miniature Shakespearean characters about the size of lead soldiers, but modelled with greater precision and beautifully coloured. Then she couldn't resist the window of the Teddy Bear Museum near Market Square.

Eventually she wandered down by the river and as she walked past the theatre something drew her towards the RSC's Bookshop in the old Victorian library building that is now part of The Swan. As she browsed idly through the books she noticed a number of biographies, she picked some up hoping to find a reference in the index to Shakespeare's childhood or early years. She glanced at *The Life and Times of William Shakespeare* by Peter Levi and Samuel Schoenbaum's *Shakespeare's Lives*. Just as she was about to leave she noticed *An ABC of Shakespeare* by Colin Duriez, and under 'Schoolmaster' she read:

> Shakespeare's first schoolmaster was probably Walter Roche. In 1571 Simon Hunt succeeded him, but retired in 1575 to attend the Catholic seminary at Douay; later he became a Jesuit. He was succeeded in 1579 by John Cottom, who remained until 1581 or 1582. By that time Shakespeare would have left school. All four masters were Oxford graduates and by the standards of the day educated men.

Thoughtfully, Anna put the book back among its companions on the shelf.

* * * * * *

Feeling relaxed after a good meal Mike and Anna left Sir Toby's early in the evening and strolled down Chapel Lane to the theatre. As they walked into the foyer they met Gillian Wykeham-Barnes, who was wearing a stunning black silk dress.

'Ah, excellent, excellent.' She spoke in her usual deep theatrical tones. 'I've just come to check that your tickets are here, before I dash off.'

'You're not staying?'

'No. I've suddenly found I could take a day off, so I'm going home to see the aged Ps. One needs to keep in touch with the family you know. So I'm off to the family domain.'

'D'you have far to go?'

'No. Just an hour or so up the M6.' She turned and looked around, 'Now let me get your tickets, I won't be a second.'

She vanished into the box office and returned with an envelope. 'There you are; enjoy your evening.'

They hardly had time to take their seats before the curtain rose on Bill Alexander's production of 'Much Ado About Nothing.'

Shakespeare had originally set the play in Italy, but it was easy to recognise the social conventions of the sixteenth century England. Kit Surrey's production was set in the secluded garden of an English country house, nestling in a topiary landscape of well-cut yew hedges. It worked well and provided a marvellous setting for the comedy.

At times it was easy to imagine that they were watching the play in the dusk of a warm summer's evening in Regents Park, except Stratford was much more comfortable.

Roger Allams' thin-skinned Benedick, took refuge behind a large moustache and a perpetual cigar. There was a marvellous moment when he was hiding in a yew tree and heard his friends talking about Beatrice's love for him. His cigar sent out agitated smoke signals as he reacted to everything they said.

Susan Fleetwood played Beatrice as a likable tomboy. Her interest in Benedick was never seriously in doubt. Benedick managed to duck her 'paper bullets of the brain' and fire off a few shots of his own, 'She speaks poniards, and every word stabs.'

Eventually Benedick and Beatrice were tricked into admitting they loved each other and danced off to get married.

Mike and Anna particularly enjoyed Dogberry, one of Shakespeare's funniest creations and, by the applause, still appreciated today.

With the audience's enthusiasm still ringing in their ears, Mike and Anna walked back towards Bull Street in silence, their minds still engrossed in the play.

Mike was the first to speak, 'I loved the phrase "paper bullets of the brain". My mind feels battered by such bullets after Bacon's *Storehouse of Formularies and Elegancies.*'

'Was the theatre too much tonight?' Anna was concerned.

'No. It was a wonderful evening. Just what my addled brain needed. The truth is I'm not used to so much scholarship. But now we must get on and solve the murders.'

Anna's mind was still in the theatre too, 'One thing about the RSC. They do everything so well — the acting, the sets, the costumes, the sword fights; I've never seen anything better. . . even the blood was so real. . .'

'Ah the *blood*. . .' They came to a sudden halt in the middle of Chapel Street. '. . .I'd forgotten about that.'

'Mmm. . ?'

'Gloria Glasspole's blood.'

'Yes. . ?'

'On your programme.'

'Yes. . ?'

'This morning the sergeant said they wanted to keep the programme a little longer.'

'Why?'

'I don't know. Except the lab-report showed it wasn't real.'

'What was it?'

'Sugar syrup.'

'*Syrup*?'

'Yes, apparently the RSC doesn't use the normal theatrical blood, *Kensington Gore*, they make their own out of sugar syrup — and that's what the police think it was.'

'Why. . ?'

'Why do they. . ?'

'No. Why should Gloria Glasspole who we know was shot, because we saw her, cover herself with stage blood? It doesn't make sense?'

'You know, I'm beginning to feel that it doesn't matter who Shakespeare's "dark lady" was; it is Gloria Glasspole that we need to look at. We should've seen it before, but the *Promus* has been "paper bullets to my brain" and it has stopped me thinking clearly.'

'So you think it is Gloria Glasspole?'

'Yep, I'm sure she's *La Belle Noire*.'

10: A WINTER'S TALE

Of all the buildings associated with William Shakespeare, the home of his mother Mary Arden at Wilmcote is probably the least known and the most interesting. The village lies a little over three miles from Stratford and the house, a Tudor farmstead, stands well back from the road behind a wall.

The two most fascinating features of the house are the kitchen and the great hall. The kitchen was dominated by a huge fire place which took up the whole width of the room and was hung with various spits and turning devices. While the 'great hall' was a bit of a misnomer, it was certainly much bigger than an ordinary room in any house of the period. It probably got its name from the fact that Robert Arden was the lord of the manor, and his status required a house with a hall.

Clyde Tombaugh was standing by the dovecote near the main entrance and was pointing out to a friend from the United States the hundreds of nesting holes. 'Don't let'm fool you,' he said. 'The sixteenth-century Brit wasn't a great bird lover. The lord of the manor was the only person in the village allowed to keep pigeons, and they would all end up on his table.'

It was mid-morning, and a tourist bus had arrived, dumping another load of dazed humanity into an ancient house already bursting at the seams with visitors.

In Stratford a similar bus had dropped another group of camera-clicking foreigners back at the Guild Chapel where, they had been told, they would see two medieval wall paintings, *Dance of Death* and *Doom*. Mike and Anna had to push their way through this crowd to get to The Prince of Denmark Hotel just a few doors further on. This time Gloria Glasspole opened the door herself; there was no sign of the dresser, and the appearance of the star had given way to a rather worried-looking actress.

Before they were seated Mike said, 'I hear the police have been to see you?'

'Yeah, that's right.'

'About the blood on your scarf?'

'Geez, ain't it a pain always being right?'

Mike let that pass, 'D'you mind telling us about it? We're still looking for the "dark lady".'

Gloria hesitated as she juggled with the confusion in her mind. 'I can't see any harm, I'd've thought everybody in Stratford knows about it by now.'

'Well we don't and it would help.'

Gloria stared at the floor, 'When Peter Warwick was holding Marco, just before you held him. . .' She looked up at Anna. 'I heard him say the "dark lady".' She paused and turned to look out of the window. 'I had an affair with Marco when he first arrived and the "dark lady" was his pillow-talk name for me. He had a thing about the sonnets, especially the raunchy bits and liked to read them to me in bed. I thought I'd be the prime suspect. . .' She paused.

'So?'

'I realised I had to change the way things looked.' She stopped again.

'And?'

'I took a gun on a late night stroll and when I was sure no one was about, I shot to look as though it'd grazed my shoulder.'

'Do the police know?'

'Sure. The Chief Inspector does. It confirmed what he'd already been told by ballistics; their report said that the shot had been fired into the shopping precinct.'

'You had a gun?' Anna looked horrified.

'Yeah, lotsa people do where I come from.'

'What did you do with it. . ?' Anna still looked appalled; but then lost her stricken look, '. . .afterwards?'

'I threw it in the river, then hauled my ass outta there. The police are trying to recover it and charge me with unlawful possession, I think that's the expression.'

'And the blood?' Mike kept the questions moving.

'I taped a plastic bag to the top of my arm containing a sponge full of it, and I punctured it at the right moment, just as we do on the stage.'

'You might've turned the searchlight away from yourself as far as the police were concerned. But it must've put you in the centre of the killer's spotlight, surely!' Mike looked aghast.

'Yeah that's what the police say.'

'And you're not worried?'

'Not really. Tomorrow's my big night, I'm playing Desdemona in Othello. And I'm as nervous as hell, so I don't have much time to think about anything else. With Marco dead Othello's going to be a mess. There's a Japanese fella playing a black guy, and lil' ol' black gal me playing a Snow Queen. . .'

'And the dustbins?' Anna still pursued her train of thought, 'We thought we heard someone knock them over as they ran away?'

'Yeah, I kicked them over to give that impression.'

'Mmm.' Mike stood and walked over to the window.

'Come on, you've gotta believe me.' The actress panicked.

Mike turned to calm her, 'Oh, I do.' He smiled trying to be as helpful as he could. 'If you'll forgive me for saying so, I think you were a fool. The police knew yesterday that the blood on your scarf wasn't real, Sergeant Williams told me.'

'So wha'do I do?'

'Get on with your work and hope that the police get the killer before he gets you.' She was far from her home and needed assistance, so Mike melted a little, 'Please phone us if we can do anything.'

'That's kind of you. I've got some of my family coming for the opening night tomorrow. Why not join us, you could meet my son, and there's a small party here afterwards, for the cast and a few friends.'

'That's very kind. Thank you.'

Having said goodbye Mike and Anna headed for the Shakespeare Centre in Henley Street, where Anna introduced Mike to Mary Black. In the entrance to the reading room, she had set out several books for Anna to see. The archivist was in her late twenties and managed to combine pretty looks with an air of serious scholarship. She leant over a table to point at a large volume, 'Here are the details of Alexander Hoghton's will.'

Anna picked it up, while Mike looked over her shoulder:

ALEXANDER HOGHTON OF LEA (3rd August 1581; proved 12th September 1581): 'In the name of God Amen. The third day of August . . . after the Incarnation of Jesus Christ one thousand five hundred and eighty-one. I Alexander Hoghton of the Lea in the county of Lancashire, Esquire, being sick of body yet of good & perfect memory, thanks be to almighty God, and considering with myself that nothing is more certain than death. . .'

They continued to look down at the page that Mary Black had pointed to.

'Item, it is my mind & will that Thomas Hoghton, my brother shall have all my instruments belonging to musics, & all manner of play clothes if he be minded to keep & do keep players. And if he will not keep & maintain players, then it is my mind that Sir Thomas Hesketh knight shall have the same instruments and play clothes. And I most heartily require the Sir Thomas to be friendly unto Fulk Gillom & William Shakeshafte now dwelling with me. . .'

Mike straightened up and for a moment kept his hand over his mouth while he thought. Eventually he said, 'Well, there is no doubt about it, in the sixteenth-century there was someone called William Shakeshafte, and he worked for Alexander Hoghton and Sir Thomas Hesketh.'

'There's no doubt is there?' Anna murmured.

'Are there any of the Hoghton family still alive today?' Mike turned to Mary Black.

'Yes. But they don't live in Hoghton Tower any longer.'

'And do the musical instruments still exist?'

'They've passed to the Heskeths, so presumably Thomas Hoghton didn't want them. The Hesketh's acquired them in the early part of the seventeenth-century and still had them in 1980. There's an inventory for Robert Hesketh dated 16 November 1620 in the county records at Preston. I've put a photocopy of it in here.' She picked up a file, 'These are for you. There's also a photocopy of Alexander Hoghton's will and details of the Hoghton family and Hoghton Tower. I should add that I don't think you'll find any other references to William Shakeshafte in Lancashire.'

She offered the file to Anna, 'That's very kind. Thank you. So all we have to do is to work out some way of connecting William Shakeshafte with Stratford?'

'Or the other way around; you could try to link Shakespeare with Lancashire?'

* * * * * *

The men from the Metropolitan Police arrived almost on the dot of 2 o'clock. They came in an unmarked car and took pleasure in parking outside the house on a double yellow line. There were three of them, all youngish sergeants, wearing dark suits and speaking with strong East London accents. Their manner gave the impression that they considered it beneath their dignity to work outside London; they declined tea and coffee.

The shorter of the three, with blunt features and the build of a boxer, took out a notebook. 'Now, we don't want to keep you waiting.' He said it in a way which implied he had no intention of being kept waiting. From time to time, a nervous twitch caused him to hold his collar down, while he pulled a face and stretched his neck. 'We've seen your statements, but we want to ask you one or two more questions.'

Occasionally he glanced at his colleagues, who

seemed happy to leave the questioning to him; so he turned in a belligerent way to Mike and Anna, 'You found the female deceased. . . er. . . Emily Lanier?'

'Yes,' Mike decided to field the questions. 'We found the body and dialled 999. There's nothing wrong with that, surely?'

'You were near, or in the vicinity of, or actually found four bodies in four days. I would've thought that that was highly suspicious, Sir.' The 'Sir' was clearly a put-down, and not politeness.

'Now, come on sergeant.' Mike wasn't going to be intimidated.

'We just happened to be there when Marco Devine and Peter Warwick were killed, and it was when we tried to find the "dark lady" that we went to Cleaver Square.'

The policeman held his collar and stretched his neck, 'I need to warn you, Sir, that we don't want you involved with any more police business. And if. . . er. . . we find that you have been, then you'll be charged with obstructing the police in the course of their duties. Is that clear?'

Mike was extremely irritated, but managed to bite back a hasty reply, 'If I hadn't gone to the War Museum after seeing the general's photograph in the flat, I wouldn't've remembered that Emily Lanier's boy friend was called Yamashita. Then we wouldn't've been able to suggest that the two crimes were connected. . .'

'I accept that, Sir, but what I'm saying is that we don't want any further initiatives of that kind. It's police business, and we'd be obliged if you'd leave it to us.'

'Talk about Neighbourhood Watch!' Mike shook his head and glanced at Anna.

'But it wasn't your neighbourhood, Sir, that's the point.'

'The police often ask for help; We were two ordinary citizens who reported what we'd seen.'

'We don't see it like that I'm afraid.'

'How do you see it?'

'As I've already said, you were involved with four

murders in less than a week, while ordinary Joe Public isn't involved in one murder in a lifetime. And not so long ago you were part of another fracas, which *also* involved drugs.'

'Ah well, You see, we don't think this is about drugs.'

'I've already pointed out that we're not particularly interested in what you think. The two cases, the recent deaths here and in London, together with what happened in Brighton last year, give us the impression that we could be dealing with gang warfare. We certainly don't want England to become another Chicago. That's why we are here. Now,' he turned to Anna. 'You seem to have a surprisingly detailed knowledge of Japanese antiques, Madam. We've been informed by our experts that your knowledge is remarkable for a member of the general public. Could you tell us how you acquired it?'

By now Anna was seething. 'Sergeant. Until a few months ago I was a teacher, surely you're not going to suggest that someone working with children could possibly. . .'

'Madam, Anthony Blunt worked at Buckingham Palace. That didn't stop him being a spy!'

Anna was speechless and attempted to regain her composure.

She took a deep breath, 'You're right; you can't presume people aren't criminals.' Then after a moment, 'I read history at university and then went on to do post-graduate studies in history of art. At the moment my special sphere of studies are the artists of the Brighton area, in particular Eric Gill. I'm writing a book about him.'

'Where does Japan come in?'

'I was coming to that. I studied at Edinburgh and St. Andrews. You may contact both Universities if you wish. One term, while I was at Edinburgh, I did a project on Japan. That's where I learnt about Japanese art.'

'Mmm.' The sergeant flicked through his notebook, 'I'm not very good with these names. . . Moter. . .'

'Mononobu.'

'Yeah Mono-whoever and Sesshu.'

'That's right. A fifteenth-century Zen priest. . .'

'You seem to know a lot about these men and their work. . .'

'It was quite fortuitous. Mononobu and Sesshu just happened to be the two Japanese artists I studied. . .'

'. . .And they just happened to be the artists whose pictures were hanging on the walls of the flat, oh come on Miss, life's not like that!'

'It's true. Check at Edinburgh. . . they were the artists in my project.'

'But you knew how they worked?'

'Of course, that's what art history is about. Anyone with a ha'porth of sense who'd studied their work would be able to describe how it was done.'

Both paused now. The interrogating policeman, anxious not to appear out of his depth turned to his colleagues. They pulled faces in reply, suggesting that he should accept Anna's explanation.

Flicking through his notebook the sergeant hastily returned to more familiar ground. It was imperative for him to regain the upper hand, 'Now, drugs. . .'

'Yes?'

'How would you describe your attitude to them?'

'In what way? Their use?'

'Yeah, let's start with that.'

'Well, obviously their misuse has grave consequences on a personal level, and they ruin health, and in a general way the pushers and users damage society. Why do you ask?'

'Y'see we found drugs at the flat in Kennington and it's the same drug that was involved in Brighton a few months ago.'

'But Michael and I had nothing to do with drugs.'

'So you say.'

'And we'll continue to say it.'

'Well, we'll accept that for a moment. But then art was also involved in Sussex.'

'Sergeant,' There was a hint of exasperation in Anna's voice. 'I'm writing a book about Eric Gill. A few months ago I was asked to look at some pictures by him. They turned out to be forgeries. While we're here in Stratford I'm finishing a book on Gill. The manuscript is upstairs if you want to see it; or write to my publishers, they'll confirm it.'

'That won't be necessary.' The sergeant closed his notebook. 'I don't think we need to take any more of your time.' With that all three policemen stood and left.

Mike and Anna watched them through the window as they got into their car and drove away. They stood speechless for some time.

Eventually Mike broke the silence, 'I think we need a cup of tea.'

'Or a strong brandy.'

'Are you serious?'

Anna laughed and shook her head, 'No, tea would be fine.' Then added, 'What *awful* men.'

Mike was stunned and still reluctant to speak as he made the tea. He poured it and sat subdued on the other side of the kitchen table from Anna. She sat with her elbows on the table, holding her cup with two hands like a bowl; she found it comforting to sip the scalding tea. Eventually she spoke looking at Mike over her teacup, 'What nasty men.'

'Mmm. But it's probably our fault.'

'How d'you mean?'

'Well, I once heard someone say that the police reflect society. Presumably things have got so bad in London that the police have been reduced to bully-boy tactics; they're *tough* police for a *tough* society.'

'You could be right, but it doesn't make them less unpleasant.'

'No. But fortunately outside London the police are still as we imagine them to be, and probably mostly in London too. We just happened to get a bad lot.'

'*And* we got a warning not to get involved.'

'It had the reverse effect on me,' Mike clenched his fists and pounded the table, 'Now I *really* want to find the "dark lady".'

'Are you serious?'

'Yes. Let's have one more try, and if we don't do it, we'll get straight back to writing.' Mike took the envelope which had arrived that morning and turned it over to make notes, 'So what have we got so far?'

'Only that Marco said "dark lady"; nothing else.'

Mike wrote it down. 'And we've still no idea who she was.'

'Oh and there's this.' Anna lifted the bottle of mineral water they had found on Marco's boat and put it in the centre of the table.

They both looked at it in silence.

'D'you know?' said Mike, 'It must be the difference between German culture and ours, but I don't think I have ever seen a less attractive bottle of water.'

'Why?'

'Well everything is wrong. . . the colour of the glass. . . the label. . . the name. . . nobody in their right mind would call something you drink 'Eau de Cologne'. Everything about it cries out, 'Don't drink me!'.'

'Maybe that's it!'

'What?'

'It's not meant to be drunk.'

'But why?'

'Because whatever is in there is more important than drinking water?'

'Mmm.' Mike looked up at Anna, 'That could be it. We must get it analysed and find out what it is.'

11: OTHELLO

The only pharmacy that Mike could remember having seen in Stratford was Boots, near the intersection of the High Street and Bridge Street; so he took the mineral water there.

Frustrated that his valuable time was being squandered satisfying a customer's curiosity rather than his need, meant that the pharmacist had only offered his services grudgingly at first. But something about Mike had caught his attention and he wrestled with the suspicion that he had seen him before. Finally the penny dropped when Mike introduced himself, and the chemist bashfully admitted that he belonged to the *Friends of the Earth*, abhorred processed food, artificial colouring and, he added with a shy smile, that his family had always enjoyed Mike's TV programmes because he promoted organically produced food.

The chemist's face almost glowed when he revealed, 'We grow all our own vegetables because we don't want anything that's been contaminated with pesticides.' He then dropped his voice to a confidential whisper, 'I'll tell you what I'll do, Mr Main.' He cradled the bottle in his arms and patted it, 'I'll take this home to my son; he's a research chemist at Aston University. I'm sure he'll run a few tests on it for you. Come back the day after tomorrow and I'll tell you what he's discovered.'

'How kind,' said Mike. 'I'm very grateful.'

'Oh, don't mention it. There are only dispensing chemists in Stratford now, and they won't be able to help you. Finding a real chemist today is very much like trying to find real food.' He raised a hand and with his chubby fingers wiggled a rather affected goodbye, 'See you in two days' time.' With that he moved off and took a prescription from another customer.

Meanwhile Anna had an idea how she could link

William Shakespeare with Lancashire and Mary Black at the Shakespeare Centre came up trumps again with a pile of books.

* * * * * *

After a light supper, Mike and Anna returned to Bull Street for a quiet evening; they settled down with coffee and Mike put on a recording of Fauré's *Requiem*. After a couple of hours, their armchairs were surrounded with a mass of books and a sea of papers. The majority of volumes scattered over the floor were either by or about Shakespeare; at a quick glance Mike appeared to be studying his plays, while Anna was absorbed with almost every available biography. When the last notes of 'In Paradisum' had died away for the second time and the the City of Birmingham Symphony Orchestra was silent, Mike got up to put on another record and he asked casually, 'Found anything?'
'Lots.'
'A connection with Lancashire?'
'I think I have.'
'Do *say*, the suspense is killing me.' Sliding the Fauré back into its sleeve, he carefully cradled Elgar's Cello Concerto between his palms, blew off the fluff and placed it on the turntable.
Anna hardly seemed to hear him; she was lost in the books open on the floor. Sucking the end of a pencil, and anxious not to lose her train of thought, she scribbled something in a notebook. 'I've just got one more piece of the jigsaw to find; when that's in place I'll be certain.'
'And it's all there in the books?'
'Every bit; and it's been there for years, but for some reason everybody's missed it.' She changed the subject, 'Oh take a look at this, it's the Hesketh inventory for 1620.' She took a photocopy from one of the pile of papers on the floor and handed it to Mike.

'vyolls, vyolentes virginalls,
sagbutts, howboies and cornetts,
cithron, flute and tabor pipes.'

Mike turned to Anna, 'What on earth is a "sagbutt"?'
'Or even "howboies"?' Anna chuckled.
Mike handed it back, 'If the truth were known, flute and virginal are about the only instruments I recognise!'
'Me too. But at least we know officially that Thomas Hoghton didn't want the *"instruments belonging to the musics"*, so they became the property of Robert Hesketh.'
'Have you found anything about the Heskeths?'
'Very little, but there's a lot on the Hoghtons.'
'Such as. . ?'
'Well they were obviously an important county family in Lancashire. . . let me find it. . . it's here somewhere.' She stooped down to another pile of papers and found the Guide To Hoghton Tower, and passed it to Mike.

The Hoghtons are descended directly from Walter, one of the companions of William the Conqueror, and through the female line from Lady Godiva of Coventry, wife of Leofric, Earl of Mercia. After the third generation from the Norman Conquest, Adam de Hoghton first assumed the family name, holding land in Hoghton in 1203.

'And you think you can link them to Shakespeare?'
'I'm sure I can. I'll know for certain tomorrow morning, when I've checked one last piece of information in the library.'
'Another coffee?'
Anna looked at her watch, 'No. I think it's time for bed.'
'I know a bank. . .'
'I knew you were going to say that!'
'Well,' he held out his hand, 'We are on a sort of honeymoon. And I think this is the evening I've always dreamed about. Marvellous music, a little gentle reading and someone to share it with. I think this is what C.S.Lewis meant when he said that married love is sometimes as comfortable as putting on your soft slippers. . .'

The unlikely thought of Mike in slippers brought a smile to Anna's face, but she was touched by her husband's contentment and his tenderness.

Mike sighed, 'The only fly in the ointment, is that we still haven't found the "dark lady".'

'I've got a funny feeling that we're suddenly going to turn a corner and walk straight into her, and she'll turn out to be — "a dark lass from Lancashire".'

'Why do you say that?'

'I don't know; call it feminine intuition.' She stood, 'Let's leave everything till the morning.'

'And so to bed. . .'

'*I know a bank. . .*' Anna quoted softly.

'*. . .where the wild thyme blows.*'

* * * * * *

'So what've you discovered?' Mike spoke as Anna got back into the car the following morning. He had stopped briefly outside the library to pick her up, and now they were on their way to Shottery for lunch.

Once seated she rubbed her hands together with delight, 'I've done it!'

'What exactly?'

'Established a link between Shakespeare and Lancashire.'

'To the Hoghtons?'

'Right onto their doorstep.'

'How?'

'Let me start at the beginning. . .'

'Do.'

'When I first thought about it, I realized that if a connection still existed today, it would probably involve one of the great families. But it's impossible to tie any of the Warwickshire families, of the sixteenth or seventeenth-century, to Lancashire; and neither the Hoghtons nor the Heskeths had any connection with Stratford. I've searched all the records, I'm certain of that. . .'

'And . . ?'

'Then I thought about vicars and curates and even bishops, but I drew a blank again. . .'

'So. . ?'

'I hit on the idea of schoolmasters. . . and bingo! should've thought of it before.' Anna clasped her hands.

'Why?' Mike had to keep his eye on the road as he looked for the turning to Shottery.

'Because John Aubrey, you remember quoted Ben Johnson and said that Shakespeare in "his younger years had been a schoolmaster in the country".'

'Of course!'

'John Cottom was the schoolmaster here in Stratford, when young master Shakespeare should've been at school.'

Mike nodded enjoying Anna's enthusiasm.

'I traced John Cottom to Oxford, Brasenose College; both he and his brother graduated there. His brother preferred a slightly different spelling of the family name, he called himself Cottam, Thomas Cottam. Then. . .'

'Uh-huh?'

'I remembered seeing a John Cottam in Alexander Hoghton's will, so I wondered if John Cottom and John Cottam were the same person. And they were!'

'You're sure?'

'Absolutely,' Anna looked at Mike. 'Joseph Gillow's *Biographical Dictionary* told me that the father of John and Thomas was Lawrence Cottam of Tarnacre in Lancashire.'

'Well?'

'The villages of Tarnacre and Lea were right next to each other, you remember that's where Sir Thomas Hesketh lived, and he was friendly with Alexander Hoghton!'

'So you think that when Alexander Hoghton needed a tutor he wrote to John Cottom in Stratford, who suggested a bright young pupil of his called *William Shakespeare*. And when William Shakespeare went to Lancashire, he called himself William Shakeshaft?

'Exactly!'

'It's a marvellous idea, but isn't it too circumstantial? You'll never be able to prove it?'

'But I *have*. . . well almost.'

'How?'

'Well I can prove that John Cottom of Stratford-upon-Avon and John Cottam of Tarnacre were the same person. And surely it's implausible that when John Cottom was away at work he knew someone called William Shakespeare, and at home he knew someone else called William Shakeshaft?'

'Highly improbable I'd've thought, but you'll still have to prove that the two Johns were the same person?'

'I've done it. I've got a copy of their signatures. One from Stratford dated 1579 and one from the Lancashire Records Office twenty seven years later, they're almost identical. There's no doubt about it, they're the same person. It's all in the records; I've done it!'

Mike went through it again in his mind.

Anna was more emphatic, 'You and Clyde said it couldn't be proved that the Stratford man, William Shakespeare, went to school and therefore it was doubtful that he'd ever have written a play. I think I've proved that he went to school. I've got documentary evidence that John Cottom, or John Cottam, of Tarnacre and Stratford-upon-Avon knew someone called William Shakeshaft who was probably a tutor in Lancashire.'

Mike realized that Anna had made her point.

They entered the tiny village of Shottery, for hundreds of years the home of yeoman farmers called the Hathaways. All over the world, the village is known as the place where you can find Anne Hathaway's cottage, which in reality is a small thatched farmstead. The oldest part of the building dated back to the fifteenth-century and today it sits in an old-fashioned English garden full of flowers.

The Hathaways actually lived in the house until the beginning of this century, and it could well have been the tide of visitors from every part of the world that finally drove them away. Visitors still come in their hordes to see the place where Shakespeare's bride lived before their marriage, and weave romantic tales about their courtship; none of which can be substantiated.

Mike and Anna paid the entrance fee and traipsed

around the cottage behind a group of Japanese schoolgirls. As always, Mike was fascinated by the kitchen; and this one with its flagged floor and oak beams was no exception. In the fireplace it was still possible to see the original bake oven, complete with a wooden door and a bread peel. After a brief look around they crossed to The Bell, the village pub, for lunch. Mike looked dejected.

'Did you find what you wanted?'

'No.'

'I'm not sure what you were looking for?'

'I'm not sure either. It was a long shot; but I suppose I was hoping to find a clue that pointed to the "dark lady".'

'And there was nothing?'

'Did you see anything?'

'Nope.'

'There you are. Clyde Tombaugh was right. The present tourist sites only have a tenuous link with Shakespeare.'

'Including Anne Hathaway's cottage?'

'Oh I think the Hathaways lived there, but that's all.

Well,' Mike rubbed his temple with his fingers, 'we've had a good try. Now I'm going back to running a restaurant and writing about food. I shouldn't've stopped in the first place.'

'What about the mineral water?'

'I'd forgotten about that. Well, I'll see if the chemist comes up with anything tomorrow; if he doesn't, then it's straight back to writing for both of us. 'I've certainly been more fortunate than you.'

'How d'you mean?'

'Well I set out to prove that Shakespeare went to school and could write, and for my money I've done that. Whereas you seem to have hit a brick wall every time you've found a clue. You've had some remarkable leads, but every time they've led you straight into a *cul de sac*.'

Mike noisily exhaled a sigh, 'It *is* surprising, isn't it? I still believe that the "dark lady" has some connection with the murders, but who she was, I've got no idea.'

'Could it be a man?'

'Possibly? Some people have always thought that the sonnets were homosexual, although A.L. Rowse insisted that they're not.'

'What were you working on last night?'

'The plays...'

'For what reason?'

'I was following up something in Alexander Hoghton's will.'

'Such as?'

'D'you remember how it began?'

'Uh-huh... with a date?'

'Yes, but there was more than that.'

'Remind me.'

'In the name of God Amen. The third day of August, after the incarnation of Jesus Christ one thousand five hundred and eighty one.'

'So?'

'It somehow suggested that the Elizabethans didn't pussyfoot around about Christianity. In their minds it was an integral part of everyday life and the way they looked at history.'

'Mmm. Fascinating.'

'So, last night I was looking at the religious thinking in the plays.'

'Is there much?'

'More than you think. And eventually I got back to the thing that keeps going around in my mind.'

'That is?'

'That a year ago I didn't really believe in Christianity, but I accepted Shakespeare as a fact. Now I regard Shakespeare as a shadowy figure who is difficult to pin-down historically, and I'm more and more convinced about Christianity.'

'So you still believe Clyde was right when he said that the Stratford man couldn't've written the plays?'

'I'm torn in two different directions. *You've* convinced me that he went to school, but Clyde is pretty persuasive too.'

* * * * * *

Later that evening when Mike and Anna had taken their seats in the theatre and glanced at the programme, Mike frowned, 'I don't think I know this play.'

Spurred by the rising buzz of excitement, Anna rushed through the bare bones of Shakespeare's tale. Expecting any moment to be silenced by the rising curtain.

'It's a simple story,' she said. 'About a black soldier from Africa who falls in love with a pretty white girl from Venice. They get married, even though her father wasn't too happy about it, but instead of living "happily ever after," the soldier becomes increasingly jealous of his wife and in the end he kills her and then himself.'

As the lights dimmed Mike whispered, 'Am I meant to enjoy it?'

Archie Lightbody's production of *Othello* was planned to be the jewel in the crown of the International Season. As the production unfolded, it was obvious that Marco's death hadn't altered that. The fact that his young Japanese understudy managed to outshine him would soon be the talk of the town.

Hitoshi Takano gave a stunning performance as Othello; he played him as a black 'Stormin Norman'. There was no sign of the rolling eyes and clicking teeth of Laurence Olivier.

Meanwhile Gloria Glasspole, captivated the audience with her Desdemona. Somehow she became a fragile peach of Italian aristocracy.

Anna was fascinated by the way the designer had managed to get the sets to look like Canaletto paintings and so made a delicate civilized city the background for a story of a soldier who lived on the raw edge of civilization. Othello appeared to control every emotion except his jealousy, the tragic flaw that finally destroyed him.

The marriage of Othello and Desdemona was a joining of minds, a love affair based an a deep understanding of each other. That made the spectacle so tragic as the audience watched Othello's jealous rage destroy the one he loved and finally himself. In the end

Mike and Anna felt sorry for Othello because he was unable to detect the evil in Iago.

They came out of the theatre knowing that they had seen a marvellous piece of entertainment which had touched the depths of human experience. Feeling elated by the drama, but subdued by the subject, they decided to give Gloria Glasspole's party a miss. On the way home they talked about the destructive nature of jealousy and the way Shakespeare set that off against the soft simplicty of a wife who was slow to see the consequences of her husband's fatal flaw.

'It's strange,' Mike put his key into the lock of 41a, 'that jealousy, unlike all the other sins, doesn't even have a moment of pleasure that can be enjoyed.'

'Mmm, that's true.' Anna paused and reflected. 'There's a lot of jealousy in the world of art too. I was thinking this morning of how G. M. Ward was jealous of Millais and when Millais first exhibited his painting of "Ophelia", Ward said a better title would be "O Failure".'

'How nasty.' Mike closed the front door. 'I think we ought to have a drink and listen to some music to clear our minds before we go to bed. I'll open some *Blanquette de Limoux*; why don't you put a record on? Elgar's Cello Concerto is still on the turntable.'

'No, after Othello we need something much bigger than that; it has to be something dramatic and heroic. What about Vaughan William's *Wasps*?'

'Just the thing. And when it's finished I'll carry you up to Puck's bank of wild and exotic herbs?'

'Why wait? We could build it down here with cushions from the sofa? 'I wonder if Vaughan Williams ever thought. . ?'

12: THE TAMING OF THE SHREW

'Ah, Mr Main there you are,' the chemist came scurrying through from the dispensary clutching the bottle. 'My wife wouldn't believe that I'd met you, nor would my son.'

'Well, I am Michael Main I promise you. We all come from the same mould, but some of us are a little bit *mouldier* than others.'

'Oh I like that Mr Main,' the pharmacist chuckled, 'And must remember it.' He handed the bottle over the counter, 'Now the contents. . . '

'Yes. . ?'

'I don't think you'll believe this.'

'Try me.'

'It's *deuterium.*'

'What?'

'Deuterium. . . y'know. . . heavy water. . . D_2O. . . I've never seen any before.'

Mike was speechless. A series of pictures flashed through his mind in a dream-like sequence: *Deuterium*. . . drugs. . . gold. . . Filipinos. . . antiques. . . the body of Emily Lanier. . . the faded photograph of General Yamashita. . . the men from the Metropolitan Police. . . Major Fergus Colerangle. . . the defiant Gloria Glasspole. . . the corpse of Marco Devine with blood seeping through the shirt. . . Peter Warwick slumped over the steering wheel of the Bugatti. What could it all mean?

As the day-dream faded he found himself still standing in Boots with the pharmacist saying, 'Mr Main. . . Mr Main. . . are you all right?'

'Er. . . yes.'

'You're sure? D'you want to sit down for a moment?'

'No. I'm fine.'

'Positive?'

'Yes, and my wife's just over there buying some moisturizer.'

In fact, Anna had moved to the check-out and turned to smile when Mike joined the queue eager to share what he had discovered, 'Any news. . .' Suddenly she looked at him, 'Is everything alright?'

'It's *deuterium*.'

'What?'

'Heavy water.'

'What's that?'

'It's used in the nuclear industry.'

'Bombs?'

'I think so.'

'Why would Marco be involved with that?'

Mike shook his head, 'I don't know. Perhaps that's what we've got to find out.'

They left Boots and went outside into Bridge Street; subdued by the discovery they walked in silence to the High Street and crossed the road.

As they passed Harvard House Clyde Tombaugh and his friend emerged. 'Hi there!' The professor's greeting brought a return to normality. Then with a note of concern the professor added, 'Are you OK Mike?'

'I think so.'

'You look as though you've seen a ghost.'

'Not a ghost exactly. . .'

'Yeah?'

'We've just been told we've got a bottle of *deuterium*.'

Clyde Tombaugh took hold of Mike's elbow, 'I think we'd better go inside.'

* * * * * *

Once they were seated in Clyde's drawing room his American friend was first to speak, 'L'me introduce myself, my name is Zygmunt Salkin, I work for the CIA. Clyde and I are old friends; I've been staying with him for a few days. At Langley we've been tracking a sample shipment of *deuterium* from the Philippines. We lost it a few days ago when the ship berthed in London.'

'So you know about it?' said Anna with a quizzical look.

'Sure. It's part of a shipment of gold and antiques being smuggled into Europe.'

'We were right then, it was gold?' Mike paused. 'And you know about Yamashita?'

'Yeah,' the man from the CIA laughed. 'But maybe I ought to ask if you mean the grandfather or the grandson?'

'What's the difference?' said Anna.

'Well, ol' grandaddy Yamashita did the burying, and the grandson is part of the gang that's digging it up.'

'So the deaths were about deuterium?'

'Hey now, young lady you're going a little too fast.'

'Anyway, Yamashita's gold has been found?'

'Yeah, that's for sure. That's where they get the money from in the Philippines to buy politicians and fix elections.'

'And we thought the deaths were about gold and antiques,' Anna shook her head.

'Well, Ma'am, that's how it all started. Then the gang gotten themselves into the Mid East.'

'I don't understand.' said Anna. 'I thought you said they came from the Far East?'

'Yeah, there's a trench in the ocean floor just off the Philippines. It's one of the deepest holes on the planet, so deep that deuterium is found there naturally. . .'

'And?'

'With modern technology, submersibles and what have you, they can bring it up to the surface. That's what the gang were going to do. At first they used the gold to finance an antiques scam, but now they're going for the big pay cheque: *deuterium*. They've invested heavily in hi-tech equipment to bring it up from the bottom of the sea.'

'What would they do with it?'

Clyde Tombaugh had been silent, but now with a glance at Zygmunt Salkin spoke up, 'There were several powers in the Middle East who want to buy their way into the nuclear club. Let's just say that if one of them could build a nuclear power station, or put an atomic bomb on top of a Scud missile, the Israelis wouldn't be too happy.

'You said 'there *were* several powers'?'

Zygmunt answered, 'Yeah, it's all become pretty hypothetical over the last few months with the collapse of the Old Soviet Block. When the Filipinos started, people were interested in the basic materials of the nuclear business. But that's no longer true; today you can buy a bomb from unscrupulous scientists from one of the old Eastern European countries; that's if the UN isn't looking. The business has gone sour on the Filipinos; but recently it's all changed again.'

'Now there's a renewed interest in "cold" fusion, and *deuterium* has become one of the most sought-after commodities in the world. It's *big* business at the moment.' He looked directly at Mike. 'Perhaps you could tell us where you found it?'

'Marco's boat.'

'Uh-huh. Where'd we find that?'

'It's moored next to the theatre.'

'Thanks. That's the help we need.'

'There're three cases of it.'

'Yeah that's what we looking for.'

'So Marco was part of all this?' said Mike.

'We only discovered that recently,' Zygmunt nodded grimly.

'When I went to the theatre in London with Ziggy,' explained Clyde, 'the night I bumped into you at Paddington, the *Evening Standard* had a front page story about the death of Yamashita in Knightbridge and his girlfriend in Kennington. I told Ziggy that she used to work here in the theatre; He put two and two together and came down to investigate.'

'We'd worked out that the Gallery Yamashita was the gang's London base, but not much more.'

'The Metropolitan Police think *we're* involved,' said Anna.

'That's my fault,' Ziggy Salkin said with a little hesitation.

'How?'

'One aspect of my work with the Agency is that sometimes we have to spread a little *disinformation*.'

'You?'

'The Japanese expert your police used in London was one of my men. We didn't know about you at the time...'

'B... but,' Anna was frantic, 'We might be charged with murder.'

'I promise that won't happen. The US Ambassador has been in touch with Scotland Yard. Your Commissioner has all the details; you won't be troubled again.'

'Marco was the leader of the gang?' Mike questioned.

'No way. He was their main courier for smuggling gold. They used his love of old cars, y'know his Bugatti; it was a great cover for the operation. He was certainly a well-paid member of the gang; that's how he managed to live in such style. But the real leader was Carlos Magenta, an old school buddy of young Yamashita.'

'Who was the killer?'

'We don't know.'

'What were the reasons for the killings?'

'Again we don't know. If we did, we might know who the killer was.'

'Hadn't we better go to the police?'

'No, I'll deal with that,' said Ziggy Salkin. 'I'll get in touch with Scotland Yard. They'll handle everything.'

'We had a visit from three very unpleasant young men from the Met,' said Anna indignantly.

'Well the police are like everybody else,' said Ziggy. 'You get the good and the bad. But I think you'll find that the Assistant Commissioner, Martin Gregory will handle this. He's a nice guy, and I bet he'll come down himself to head up the operation.'

'So,' said Mike getting to his feet, 'That's it. Mr Salkin you've certainly taken a load of my mind. I feel a sense of relief that you obviously know what you're doing. I think we should leave everything in your capable hands.'

With that Mike and Anna took their leave and with much lighter hearts were soon back in the over crowded High Street of Stratford-upon-Avon.

* * * * * *

'Well, well,' murmured Mike filling the kettle for coffee once back at Bull Street. 'Things are beginning to fall into place.'

'In one sense that's true.' Anna got the mugs and added coffee, 'but in another, we still don't know who the "dark lady" was.'

'I've been thinking. . .'

'Yep. . ?'

'What if we are dealing with two totally different issues?'

'Mike, what are you talking about. . ?'

'Suppose there was the smuggling and. . ?'

'Mmm?' Anna tried hard to make sense of what Mike was saying.

'Well. . . last night?'

'*Othello*?'

'Yes. . . the whole point of the play.'

'What in particular?' Anna looked blank.

'Sexual jealousy?'

'Mike, that can't be relevant. How could that possibly fit in with gold, antiques and. . . er. . . heavy water?'

'It doesn't.'

'But. . .'

'Think of the smuggling as something completely separate. Then imagine that lover boy, Marco Devine upset a ladyfriend who in a fit of jealous rage killed him. . . and Peter Warwick too. . . because, he knew all about her. . . whoever she was.'

'And Emily Lanier?'

'Yes, and her boyfriend as well, if he knew too much.'

'I suppose it's possible?'

'Come on. . . it's *more* than that.'

'So, Mike who was it?'

Very slowly and very quietly he said, 'Gillian Whykeham Barnes. . . ?'

'Mike, that's *ridiculous*. . .'

'I wish it was. The trouble is you don't want to think that Gillian could be involved. But it seems to me that she could well be part of this whole sorry business.'

'How?'

'D'you remember that photograph of Yamashita?

Well, there's another one. I can see it now, it was on Marco's boat.'

Anna felt that she must hold on to Gillian's innocence. 'There were lots of photos on the boat. . .'

'Yes, but one in particular, taken somewhere in the Carribean, the girl was in a bright green swimming. . .'

'And sun glasses, with snorkelling equipment; Mike I do remember. I can see it too.' Anna paused with a hand over her mouth. 'And I remember. . .'

'Go on.' Mike was encouraged that Anna had at last caught his train of thought.

'There's something about *Hoghton Tower*, that's linked to her as well. . .' She picked up the file of material she had collected on William Shakeshafte and flicked through the papers, 'Yes, here it is,' She read from: *The Official Guide to Hoghton Tower*. 'Hoghton Tower (Just off the M6). Is the family home of the Hoghton's. They are descended from Walter one of the companions of William the Conqueror, and through the female line from Lady Godiva. . .' She suddenly looked dispirited, 'No I was wrong, there's nothing here.'

'Wait a moment. There *is*, the M6.' Mike was fairly jumping at this stage. 'I think we'll discover that Gillian's home *is* Hoghton. . .'

'Now we're getting somewhere! Let's phone the theatre and check. . .' Anna picked up the phone and dialled the number, 'Hello. . . Miss. . . er. . . Wykeham-Barnes please. . . she's. . . where. . ? Hoghton?' She turned to Mike and raised her eyebrows in amazement, 'Yes, I've got that Hoghton. . . H-O-G-H-T-O-N. . . in Lancashire. When d'you expect her back? Five. . . for the back stage tour. . . Thank you, goodbye.'

As she put the 'phone down Anna didn't know if she felt elated or sad; had they found the "dark lady" at last? But if it was Gillian, then it was a terrible discovery. 'Do you think we've solved it?' She turned to Mike.

'I think so. Somehow, Gillian Wykeham-Barnes is the "dark lady".' Mike looked at his watch, 'And in less than an hour we'll be able to confirm it.'

'Should we phone the police?'
'Certainly we ought to let Ziggy Salkin and Clyde Tombaugh know.'

* * * * * *

Mike had bought tickets for the backstage tour from the counter in the RSC bookshop, and then joined Anna near the entrance to the Swan Theatre, where the group of Japanese schoolgirls that they had seen at Shottery was already waiting. Within seconds Clyde Tombaugh and Ziggy Salkin arrived, quickly followed by Sergeant Percy Williams.

He spotted Mike and Anna and came over. 'I'm glad I've seen you, do you happen to know anyone called Salkin?'

'Yes, he's right here,' Mike introduced them.

'We've had a call from Scotland Yard, Sir,' the Sergeant explained to Ziggy. 'The Assistant Commissioner is on his way. I've been asked to make contact with you. My boss is at a conference in Birmingham at the moment, so I'm to be your liaison with the local force. I confess I'm not sure what all this is about.'

'Well Sarge, we're interested in Marco Devine because he was involved with a gang smuggling gold, stolen antiques and...'

'Drugs..?'

'No, Sarge not drugs. They're certainly part of the gang's operation in the East, but not in Europe. Its a drugs-free scam here at the moment, but recently the gang has moved into heavy water, and samples arrived in Britain a few days ago. That's why the CIA are interested. Mr Main has located it for us.'

'Really?' The sergeant blinked in disbelief.

'Yes. With Mr Main's help, we've found the samples, three cases labelled *Eau de Cologne*...'

'They were on Marco's boat...'

'That's right Sergeant, and now they are in the trunk of my car. Apart from one bottle opened for analysis they're all intact. Would you like me to sign for them?'

'That won't be necessary, Sir. But, if we're here for the heavy water, why are we in the theatre and not at the boat?'

'Because Mr and Mrs Main have probably found your killer too.'

'And who would that be, Sir?' The sergeant now looked quite peeved.

'Gillian Wykeham-Barnes,' said Mike.

'Miss Wykeham-Barnes?' the sergeant exploded.

'Yes,' said Mike, 'we think it could be; and she'll be here any second to lead the backstage tour.'

At precisely that moment Gillian's assistant appeared. 'Those for the backstage tour,' she announced, 'this way.' She led them into the empty foyer of the Swan Theatre. 'We are a working theatre and the stages have been set for tonight's performances, so please don't touch anything. I will point out the things of interest as we go around.' Her mind switched to automatic as the much repeated monologue ground its way to the surface of her subconscious. She thought of one way to relieve the monotony, 'Are there any questions?'

'I thought that Miss Wykeham-Barnes was going to lead this tour,' said Clyde Tombaugh.

'I'm her assistant; she's asked me to do it for her. Veronica Jewsbury's my name; Miss Wykeham-Barnes is just back from a day off and has some important papers to deal with.'

'So she is back?'

'Absolutely. She'll have a few words to say at the end of the tour.' At this, Miss Jewsbury shot off at great speed into the Swan Theatre with everybody trailing behind.

The Swan's auditorium is small, and there is no proscenium arch, so the audience sits on three sides of the stage; it is theatre in the round and at its most intimate. Veronica Jewsbury mounted the stage and with both hands made a sweeping gesture that encompassed the whole building. 'You are standing in what was the shell of the original theatre destroyed by fire in 1926. It was always the RSC's intention to rebuild it, but the necessary funds were never available. That is, not until 1982 when Frederick Koch, an American visitor who was looking around the theatre just like you, wrote out a cheque and handed it to us. That gave us the Swan as you see it today, enabling us to experience theatre very much as they did in Shakespeare's time.'

One of the Japanese school girls interrupted, 'How much please?'

'How much did it all cost? Oh I don't think that has ever been made public. Let's just say if you were talking in dollars, then you'd be talking in millions rather than thousands. Does that answer your question?'

The girl nodded.

'Good,' Another sweeping gesture followed as she pointed at the back wall. 'On the other side of that wall is the main theatre, so you see we don't have much room. Follow me.'

Again everybody moved off at great speed, this time through a connecting door which led into the backstage area next door. Once through, the tour party assembled by the props table and peered at the items set for that evening's performance. There were little leather purses with draw-strings full of gold coins, letters in elegant Elizabethan copperplate that looked as though they had been written with a goose quill on parchment. There were lanterns and keys. Next to the table was the rack of swords in their scabbards, standing in what appeared to be an old umbrella stand.

There was a gentle murmur of excitement as the young Japanese girls pressed forward to see the objects that their heroes and heroines would soon carry onto the stage. They had been forbidden to touch, but longed to do so, imagining that these objects were touchstones that would immediately connect them to what in their minds was the magical and glamorous world of the theatre.

They heard Gillian's voice as she came down the stairs from her office. She had her back to them as she came into view and was still calling to someone above, 'No. I need six seats for tonight. Would you see that they are left at the box office in the name of Harrison. They're for the party from the Arts Council.' Shuffling through some papers as she turned to speak to Veronica Jewsbury, she was surprised to find herself confronted by Mike, Anna, Clyde, Ziggy and the sergeant.

The atmosphere was immediately charged with such tension that the schoolgirls were suddenly silenced and turned to see what was happening. Several seconds passed when nobody moved or said anything.

Gillian suddenly hissed in their direction, 'Get out of here.'

'Wha. . ?' Was all Anna managed.

Then a loud and commanding Lancastrian voice said, 'Don't move.' And in a single fluid movement Councillor Bertram Norris stepped in front of Gillian Wykeham-Barnes and grabbed a sword from the rack, flicked its scabbard into the dark space of the auditorium, took hold of a young Japanese girl as a shield and backed down stage towards the footlight. 'I think you were about to hear from Miss Jewsbury that they use real swords at the Royal Shakespeare Company. But if you move you'll discover that in a much more unpleasant way.'

The Councillor suddenly looked at Ziggy Salkin whose hand had slowly slipped into his jacket to reach for the gun under his arm. 'I thought I said don't move?' He tightened his grip on the petrified schoolgirl. 'I don't know who you are but if I see you move again, this child will get her throat cut. . . is that clear?' You could almost hear the Japanese girls gulp, as he threatened to harm their companion.

'Yes, I understand.' Clyde Tombaugh's American friend annunciated slowly and clearly. 'My name is Zigmunt Salkin; I'm with the CIA. I am also at a disadvantage. I don't know who you are?'

Bertram Norris drew himself to his full height behind his human hostage and looked down his beaked nose, 'My name is Bertram Norris. A name that'll soon be linked forever with the author of these magnificent plays. And then the farce of thinking they ever had anything to do with that nobody called Shakespeare will be over for good.'

'You. . . m. . . must be out of your mind, 'Clyde Tombaugh stuttered.

'My God! Look whose talking? Think of the thousands of hours wasted every year by those who churn out millions of words and who never get within a whisper of naming the real author?'

Ziggy Salkin had obviously been trained in hostage strategy and he continued to speak slowly and quietly, 'So, you know who the real author was?'

'You bet your bottom dollar I do.'

Anna spoke up, 'He thinks it was Edward de Vere.'

'. . .Don't be so bloody silly lass. That was a put-up-job to keep you off the scent. There's no chance that the plays were written by a de Vere. They're the work of great genius and the de Vere family could never produce that in a thousand years.'

'OK,' Ziggy Salkin inched further forward. 'So you know who wrote the plays,' he was playing for time. He had no idea what he was going to say next, but was hoping that Clyde Tombaugh would speak. 'Well I thought they were written by a guy called Shakespeare?' In his mind he was willing Clyde to say something relevant; something erudite about Shakespeare. 'I thought three hundred years ago someone actually called him. . .' What was it Clyde had said? Shake. . . Shake stage. . ? Shake-light? Why, why, *why* didn't Clyde speak?

'. . .Shake-scene.' Yes, that was it; that's what Clyde had said the other evening. 'And in saying Shake-scene he confirmed it was Shakespeare who had written the plays?'

'When Robert Greene said that he wasn't referring to Shakespeare. . .'

At last Clyde Tombaugh's inquisitiveness as a scholar made him speak, 'Why d'you say that?'

'What! Has the great Shakespearian authority missed something?' He continued to look down his nose with contempt as he clutched the girl still tighter.

'Obviously; because I don't follow?'

'When Robert Greene mentioned "Shake-scene." He couldn't've been speaking about Shakespeare...'

'Why..?'

'Why don't scholars ever look at the evidence..?'

'But..?'

'When Greene's diatribe was published in September 1592; nobody had really heard of Shakespeare...'

'1592? Mmm... 1592; yeah you could be right..?'

'Of course I'm right. Greene was talking about Edward Alleyne...'

Mike had tried to follow, 'Edward who..? That doesn't make any sense?

'Of course it does laddie. "Shake-scene" was a normal Elizabethan way of talking about an *ac-torr*...'

'So who wrote the plays?' Ziggy edged closer.

'Christopher Marlow...'

'That's absurd,' said Anna. 'He died in 1593; everybody knows that.'

The Councillor droned on, 'He faked his death so he could live with his patron-lover Thomas Walsingham in Chislehurst. It was there that he secretly wrote the plays; and Thomas Walsingham was the "dark lady" of the sonnets...'

'You're sick,' said Anna.

'That's what Marco said.' He pulled the girl still closer. 'I wanted to read the sonnets to him and love him. And in the end Marco would contemptuously spit the words "dark lady" at me every time we met. That's why I killed him...'

Ziggy was within striking distance, 'So you...'

There was a commotion at the back of the theatre; a door burst open and the sudden pool of light revealed half a dozen policemen rushing into the back of the auditorium.

'Stay where you are,' one called.

Councillor Norris, had now lost his only way of escape, so he moved to the other side of the stage. Still clutching the schoolgirl, he pushed her up a spiral staircase that led up into the flies and a mass of lighting gantries.

Ziggy Salkin had drawn his gun, the party of schoolgirls, looked terrified and backed into the shadows. But curiosity overcame their fear and they peered out determined not to miss any of the real-life drama that was unfolding before them.

The Assistant Commissioner, Martin Gregory, led a small armed group of crouching policemen through the back stalls. 'Give us more light!' he shouted.

'Lights, more lights,' echoed Sergeant Williams.

The stage was immediately flooded with a blinding glare that had the reverse effect; it was now impossible to see anything.

'There he is!' a policeman pointed. His voice broke the eerie silence hanging over the stage as everyone struggled with temporary blindness.

The Councillor was crossing a walkway high in the flies. The shout made him hesitate; he tripped and fell towards the stage. The schoolgirl he had been holding also fell and screaming, managed to grab a rail of lights and hang on.

Had it been a summer's day, and had Bertram Norris been diving into a pool, his body would have entered the water with hardly a splash. He died instantly as his body struck the stage; his neck took the full force of the impact. He had extended his arms to brake the fall, but from that height it was of little use.

The few moments of stunned silence were followed by an explosion of activity as everyone rushed to help the swinging figure of the child still clutching at the lighting rig.

Sergeant Williams was first below her, he held out his arms and coaxed her, 'Let go! You'll be all right!'

She cried out in Japanese as her fingers lost their grip; then dropped safely into his arms. With relief her school friends rushed to her side.

All this had taken the focus off the Councillor's crumpled body. Martin Gregory clambered onto the stage and called to one of his men, 'See to that, will you?' He looked around.

'Ah there you are Mr Salkin.' He spotted Ziggy, who

was returning his gun to its holster. 'Yes, I think you'd better put that away.'

'Thanks for coming,' Ziggy shrugged to adjust his jacket so that the bulge of the gun wouldn't show.

When everybody had rushed to Percy Williams and the young girl, Anna had crossed the stage to Gillian Wykeham-Barnes still standing at the bottom of the stairs. Somehow she had become rooted to the spot by the sheer horror of all that had happened.

They took hold of each others hands. Then Gillian pulled herself away, 'You thought is was me didn't you?'

'Yes, I did.'

'I could see that, when I turned around at the bottom of the stairs.'

'But I'm relieved it wasn't,' Anna sighed and smiled.

'In a way I was involved. I fell for Marco when he first arrived. He worked out my family's connection with Hoghton. I told him my mother's family believed we were all descendants of the illegitimate child of Shakespeare and Alexander Hoghton's niece, that she was Shakespeare's first love and "dark lady" of the sonnets. I had an affair with Marco until I realized he wasn't in love with me. He was in love with an idea; he was excited by the thought he was making love to a relative of the "dark lady".'

Anna shook her head at their blindness in not spotting the Hoghton connection sooner, 'And that painting of Lady Godiva in your office. We missed that too.'

'Mmm, the last of the family's treasures,' Gillian spoke quietly and with a tinge of regret.

When Mike and Clyde joined them, Anna was still shaking her head in disbelief at their incompetence, 'So it was Bertram Norris?'

'He's quite mad you know,' said Gillian. 'That's why I shouted at you. He had come to my office and said he had a document that proved Christopher Marlow was the author of the plays.'

'Surely, that's not possible?' said Anna.

But Clyde Tombaugh was nodding in agreement, 'There is a theory that's gaining ground at the moment. . .'

'Hang on,' said Mike with disbelief. 'Christopher Marlow was killed in a pub fight?'

'As Bertram Norris said,' Clyde continued. 'That could simply be what we're supposed to think. Some people say Marlow fixed his own disappearance. He knew that the officers of the crown were closing in. So he wrote himself out of the script.'

'Why?'

'His homosexuality and atheism were capital offences.'

'What happened to him?'

'Well, he could've lived secretly in Chislehurst writing the plays we know as Shakespeare's. The Councillor was right he had the intellectual genius and the stage-craft to do it.'

Mike frowned, 'Shake-scene; what was that all about?'

Clyde Tombaugh was now in his element, 'Just before a rather unhappy actor called Robert Greene died in 1592, he wrote something called, "A *Groatsworth of Wit*" in which he was sarcastic about another actor, whom he described as an "upstart crow" and "Shake-scene". . .'

'Again Councillor Norris was right. If he wrote that in 1592, it is highly unlikely he was referring to Shakespeare. . .'

'So Bertram Norris was the killer,' said Anna. 'And it was sexual jealousy too?'

'I should've spotted that,' said Gillian. They all turned to her. 'There've been rumours for sometime about a local homosexual chasing Marco. And he would have none of it. Marco was one of those men who are aggressively heterosexual; he even went as far as making fun of those who aren't. It is certainly possible that Bertram Norris killed him in a fit of jealousy; the Councillor was a very violent man.'

'This might help?' The Assistant Commissioner had been speaking to a group of police near the body, but now came to join to them with a letter in his hand.

'What is it?' said Mike.

'One of my men has just found it on the body. It is a

'One of my men has just found it on the body. It is a letter from Marco Devine. In no uncertain terms, he told Bertram Norris to get lost. He denied that there's any possibility that the sonnets were homosexual. And he ends by saying that he'd never be Bertram Norris's "dark lady".'

Ziggy Salkin stepped forward, 'Commissioner, l'me introduce you to Mr and Mrs Main, I should've done it sooner.'

'I'm glad to meet you,' said Martin Gregory. 'I was born in Sussex, so I know Kings Nympton. In fact I've had many delightful meals in your restaurant. I hope you haven't given it up?'

'No. No.' Mike reassured him, 'We've only recently married, and we didn't get too much time off after the wedding, so we've come to Stratford for a little holiday and to do some writing. . .'

'About food I hope?'

'I am, but Anna is writing about Eric Gill. . .'

'The Ditchling man?'

'That's right,' said Anna. 'You know him?'

'Indeed I do. I've got two beautiful woodcuts of his and a wood carving by his nephew, John Skelton. He must live quite near you?' He paused. 'Now we'd better get all this wrapped up so they can put on the show tonight.' He turned and spotted Percy Williams, 'Sergeant, is your chief coming?'

'It's Sergeant Williams, Sir, Percy Williams.' He came smartly to attention. 'Mr Good's in Birmingham for a conference. He asked me to deal with whatever is necessary.'

'Well I'll leave everything in your hands. . . there'll need to be a post mortem.'

'Of course, Sir. I'll see to that.'

The Assistant Commissioner turned to Ziggy. 'We've arrested the four junior members of the gang in London. Is there anything I can do for the CIA before I go?'

'I've got a sample of heavy water. May I keep it?'

'Please do. I'll be sending a report to the Chief of Police in Manila. I'll tell him you've got it, and I'll impress on him that he must deal with Carlos Magenta and the rest of the gang.'

The centre of the stage became like the eye of a storm. The London policemen had removed the body; the Japanese school girls had been taken back to their hotel; and the theatre staff were struggling to get everything ready in time. Mike, Anna, Clyde, Ziggy, the Assistant Commissioner and the sergeant were aware of immense activity elsewhere, but they were in a place that was suddenly very still and quiet.

* * * * * *

Mike and Anna walked back towards Bull Street in silence.

'I feel terrible,' said Anna. 'That I even thought it was Gillian?'

'So do I,' said Mike. He suddenly stopped in the middle of the road. 'Will you promise me something?'

'I'll try. . .'

'Don't *ever* let me get involved with anything like this again!'

'Mmm.'

'From now on, my only interests are going to be food, food and nothing but food.' Mike laughed. 'And y'know suddenly I don't even feel hungry.'

They were soon enveloped in the crowds that usually fill the streets of the little Warwickshire town of Stratford-upon Avon.

'Do you still think that Shakespeare didn't write the plays?'

'D'you know I don't know? And I don't really care; whoever wrote them was a genius, and we can enjoy them today. That's the important thing.'

They walked into Bull Street, 'On second thoughts, I think we might have a little food tonight. A light supper; something Old English is called for — even Elizabethan.'

'Such as?'

'Oh I don't know, "*ox-pith on toast*", or even "*fysshe of*

the mountayn", or perhaps "*cockatrice on a bed of peggles*". . .'
'What on earth is that. . ?'
'You wait and see.'

END